THE PERFECT PUDDING
– A Space Adventure

THE PERFECT PUDDING
– A Space Adventure

Fiona C Ross

Spiderwize

The Perfect Pudding - A Space Adventure

Spiderwize
Office 404, 4th Floor
Albany House
324/326 Regent Street
London
W1B 3HH
UK

www.spiderwize.com

ISBN: 978-1-908128-23-2

For Grace, Sam and Matt xxx

Special thank you to

Gale Winskill (www.winskilleditorial.co.uk)

Shilpashree Balaram – illustrations

Helen Elizabeth Ramsey

Jane Sharman

Contents

Background to the Story

The Perfect Pudding is set in the Earth year 3050. Life has been discovered on many planets in the Milky Way Galaxy and beyond. Instant translation devices make communication easy for all.

Introducing

Flo, Hugo, Hector and Jemima Potati, a family passionate about space travel from Planet Uz in the Andromeda Galaxy

A waiter at The Crater Café on Mercury

Val, a volcanologist and pancake maker on Venus

Elena from the Amazon Rainforest on Earth

The Martian Marshmallow Maker on Mars

Jax, a slush-maker on Saturn's tiny ice moon

A bunch of Jovians working in Space TV

Flo

Hugo and Jemima

Hector

1

Flo's Great Idea

"You eat it dear," Jemima smiled handing her daughter the last jammy cream in the packet.

Flo Potati looked at the stale biscuit in her mother's long, green fingers and sighed. "Let's half it," she suggested, breaking it in two and giving her a piece.

"Well, maybe just a nibble," Jemima agreed, biting off a crumb and handing it back to Flo.

Things had been like this for a while on the Potati family's spaceship. Since leaving Planet Uz in the Andromeda Galaxy for the Milky Way, food had been in short supply and everyone was hungry all the time.

"Dad, where's your big toe?" Flo gasped when she saw her father trying to slide his slipper on before anyone noticed the missing digit on his left foot.

"It's okay, dear," Hector assured her. "It'll grow back when we get more food."

That was little comfort to nine-year-old Flo, and when her father's right ear fell off and landed on his lap after a measly meal of dry crackers she knew things were reaching crisis point. She could hear her parents' anxious chatter late into the night.

"We should have planned better for the journey," Jemima muttered. Hector tried to take the blame by saying things like, "It was my fault for eating too much at the start of the journey when the cupboards were stocked with food."

But Jemima wasn't having any excuses.

"We've put our children's health at risk," she blubbered. "Travelling for weeks to find a friendly planet to get supplies, and even then we aren't getting nearly enough."

Hector blamed himself for that too. He spent most of his time working on inventions to exchange for any food they could get, but his inventions weren't working as well as they used to, and his ideas were getting rather dull.

"The *smelly-vision's* quite good," Jemima said encouragingly.

"But useless if you don't have a nose," Hector reminded her.

"And the *dream machine* is always entertaining," she lied.

"We'll give up space travel," Hector resolved, "At least until the children are older and settled safely into space college."

"We'll have to," Jemima agreed. "It's the best thing."

Flo's younger brother, seven-year-old Hugo Potati, was as concerned as his sister about their parents' health.

"Did you see the size of their dinner portions?" he said to her one evening, after hurrying into her bedroom for a natter.

"They were microscopic," Flo agreed, switching on her computer for her usual surf of the Space Web before bed.

"They give *us* food to keep up *our* strength, but meanwhile they're fading away," Hugo sniffed, wiping tears from his eye. "Mum's arm has lost four inches, at least."

"That much?" Flo gasped in dismay. "How will she be able to fly the spaceship if the controls are out of her reach?"

"I know," Hugo whimpered. "I saw her with a pole earlier trying to reach the button for the autopilot."

Both Flo and Hugo knew that when food was short an Uzian's body disintegrated in an attempt to save energy and preserve life. But this was the first time they had seen it happen and the effects were rather horrifying.

"They've been talking about giving up space travel," Flo whispered, not wanting her parents to overhear their worries.

"No!" Hugo gasped, appalled at the thought of it. He loved exploring the galaxies just as much as everyone else in his family. "Do you think we'll last until we get to the Food and Fun Fest?" he said, grabbing a cushion and lying down on the bed.

"*We'll* be fine," Flo assured him, "But I don't know about Mum and Dad."

The Food and Fun Fest was held every year on the Dog Bone Asteroid.[1] It was a great day out for families to exchange whatever they had for whatever they needed, and the Potatis always relied on it to stock up their kitchen cupboards.

"But I don't think we can depend on the success of their inventions this year," Flo said in a low voice. "I've heard

---

[1] Also known as *Asteroid 216 Kleopatra.*

Mum and Dad complain about them and now they don't have the energy to do final tests and trials."

"I don't want to set up home on a planet or moon because we don't have enough food and energy for space travel," Hugo sighed wearily. "And anyway, how would Mum and Dad cope with 'real' jobs rather than working on their wacky inventions? You know how hard it is to get them out of bed most mornings."

"Some days they don't even bother getting out at all," Flo reminded him. "I want us to have bundles of energy and everything we need to travel to wherever we want," she said getting up from her seat.

"So ... any ideas?" Hugo said, looking up at his sister.

"I have one," Flo said taking her brother's slimy hand and leading him over to her bedroom window.

"Just imagine," she began, "If I could make a pudding; a pudding with unique and sensational flavours that everyone wanted a slice of. We could exchange *that* at the Food and Fun Fest for whatever we needed to continue with our space travels."

"But how can you make a pudding without any ingredients?" Hugo asked, liking the idea but not thinking it possible.

"We have to look *beyond* our empty kitchen cupboards," Flo smiled, thinking through her plan.

"To where?" Hugo asked baffled.

"To *there*," Flo said pointing at the bright light in the black sky.

Hugo stared at Planet Mercury in the distance.

"According to my navigational device we'll be there in the morning," Flo said with a confidence that took even her by surprise. "And that, my little brother, is where I'm going to get the first ingredient for the Perfect Pudding."

"The Perfect Pudding," Hugo repeated slowly, thinking about the name.

"I've been doing some research on the Space Web and there are some amazing ingredients in the Milky Way Galaxy," Flo told him, watching the sparkle slowly return to his eye.

"But how are you going to get them?" Hugo asked, deciding he liked the idea *and* the name.

Flo slid her long, windy arm under her bed and pulled out a box of her parents' inventions.

"Paper with Flavour and *Hector's Beards,"* she said, blowing away the space dust and lifting the lid with her twenty bony fingers. "Some of this stuff's not too bad," she grinned, hanging a beard from her large, pointed ears and popping a strip of *Paper with Flavour* between her dry, scaly lips. "If I can somehow convince everyone that these things are, in fact, the best thing since freeze-dried dumplings and vacuum-packed sausages, we can trade our parents' inventions for ingredients for the Perfect Pudding."

"Do you really think there's any chance of that?" Hugo said doubtfully.

"Possibly not ... but we've got nothing to lose," Flo reminded him.

2

Hugo the Designer and Advertiser

The idea of creating "the Perfect Pudding" had been on Flo Potati's mind long before things began to get unpleasant for her family. At the start of their travels when the kitchen cupboards were full, Flo had gone wild in the kitchen, making all sorts of delicious and imaginative treats for her family to enjoy. She discovered she had a passion for cooking; a flair for combining ingredients and creating exciting new flavours. As her filo pastry was crispy yet succulent and her soufflé rose to perfection she made up her mind that, one day, she would be a top chef. She also decided to test her skills to the limit and take on the ultimate cooking challenge. She would make a pudding that was *perfect*.

Hector and Jemima were usually too busy in the spaceship's Inventing Room or flying the spaceship to extend *their* creative talents to the kitchen.

"What do you call these again?" Hector asked one evening when Flo invited everyone into the kitchen to sample her latest creations.

"Lemon naffs," Flo said, watching her father lick the sticky cream with his long, spiky tongue; "A cross between a lemon paff and a lemon noffle."

"Quite ingenious," Hector drooled, "*And* delicious."

"These are divine," Jemima slavered, wrapping her forked tongue around a jammy space puff.

"I could eat this all day," was her brother's reaction to just one nibble of the raspberry ripple.

But as they got further into their space travels and the kitchen cupboards began to empty, Flo was told to cut down on her delicious treats.

Hector and Jemima had been shocked when they discovered the extent of the problem.

"I hope we last until the Food and Fun Fest!" Jemima said in tears when she realised they hadn't landed on a friendly planet for the best part of two million light years.

"We will if we're careful," Hector assured her, counting out slices of vacuum-sealed bread rolls for dinner. "But definitely no more treats. Portions will be measured and the kitchen will be locked during the day to resist temptation."

Flo's creativity in the kitchen was stopped and she knew without a whisper of doubt she was the one responsible for the terrible mess they were all in. Her idea to create the Perfect Pudding was put on hold, until the night she read about the wonderful ingredients in the Milky Way Galaxy.

"You'll need a designer," Hugo said when he realised his sister was serious about creating the taste sensation. "You might be great with flavours and texture, but a pudding needs *style*. It needs to be appealing to the eyes *and* to the taste buds."

"Sounds good!" Flo agreed surfing the Space Web. She had read about a place called The Crater Café on Mercury and was busy trying to find a detailed map to plan her route. She couldn't risk relying on satellite navigation alone.

"I'll draw up some ideas anyway," Hugo said, aware he didn't have his sister's full attention. "Along the lines of the best way to present a pudding on a plate, and what a perfect pudding should look like. *And* you'll also need me to work on the advertising side of things."

"Advertising?" Flo said, printing off a map of the heavily cratered flatlands. "Why do we need to work on *that*?"

"To convince the customers to taste the pudding at the Food and Fun Fest, of course," Hugo said writing his first thoughts in his notebook. "You can't assume that everyone will want to taste your pudding just because you *tell* them it's perfect. What if they don't believe you? *Why* should they believe you?"

"I hadn't thought of that," Flo said folding up her map and sliding it into the groove behind her left ear. "We must think of everything we can to ensure we have the best chance of continuing with our space travels. By the way ... something I forgot to mention," she said, watching her brother at work. "The Perfect Pudding must remain a secret."

"Why?" Hugo asked, putting down his pencil and looking at her.

"Because Mum and Dad will eat the ingredients," Flo said knowingly. "I saw Dad on his hands and knees earlier searching the spaceship for crumbs. If he knows what I'm planning to stash under my bed, there'll be no stopping him."

"I won't say a word," Hugo nodded, getting back to work.

"I'll try to get some extra ingredients if I can," Flo said, checking that the box of *Paper with Flavour* and *Hector's Beards* were dust-free and ready to go. "We'll have a treat when I get back from the planets to restore everyone's energy, but most of the ingredients will stay hidden until we touch down on the Dog Bone Asteroid."

"So what are you planning to get on Mercury?" Hugo asked as Flo headed to the door.

"Well ... the nippy cinnamon sauce sounds amazing and the asteroid meringues sound fabulous," Flo smiled, "But I *really* want to taste the hot ice cream."

"*Hot* ice cream!" Hugo muttered grabbing his pencil. "How can ice cream be hot?"

"It's heated by the Sun," Flo told him, stuffing the box under her arm. "Tastes like ice cream, but it's really a delicious, sweet sauce."

"That could go with any pudding!" Hugo exclaimed, opening his sketch pad. "It could be drizzled on top of a pudding or dotted around the plate, or even poured along the side of the pudding. Yes, I like the idea of hot ice cream," he smiled, turning his pad to show his sister his ideas, but she was already gone.

"Heat-resistant metal. The finest there is!" Hector assured his daughter as she loaded the box of *Paper with Flavour* and *Hector's Beards* into the space pod and got ready for take-off.

"I just hope I can find a smooth surface to land it!" she beamed as the hatch on the roof of the spaceship slid open and she stared down at the holey planet. The solar panels on top of the pod's wings were instantly charged by the bright sunlight, and with a glance over her shoulder at her parents and brother, who were waving and shouting "good luck", she steadied her nerves and flew out of the spaceship into the black sky.

3

Hot Ice Cream

Planet Mercury's North Pole was a lot bigger than it looked on the map and if the pod's satellite navigation system hadn't eventually picked up the Crater Café Flo knew she would have been lucky to find it. Mercury had looked *holey* from the spaceship window, but now that she was trying to land the pod she realised there were very few places that were not covered in craters. It was as if someone had got hold of a giant wooden spoon and beaten big dents into its roasting-hot crust.

The café was the perfect resting place after the long flight. Flo sat back in her rock chair and studied the menu. The nippy cinnamon sauce, the asteroid meringues and the hot ice cream were all on it. She would also taste the comet surprise just to be sure she had the best ingredient for the Perfect Pudding. It all depended on one thing.

"You would look fantastic with a beard!" she said to the waiter pulling out an extra curly black one from her box.

"A what?" the waiter said, straightening the menus, and staring suspiciously at the thing in Flo's hand.

"A *beard*," Flo repeated. "They're all the rage on Planet Earth. You stick it on your face."

"Sounds ghastly," the waiter shuddered. "I always wondered about those Earthlings."

"Is it alive?" he asked, leaning forward to get a better look at the beard. "Perhaps it's a cat," he smiled, stroking it gently. "I've read about cats. I wouldn't mind one to keep me company on the long, cold nights."

"No, it's a type of hair," Flo told him dangling it from her ears. "You can cut it into any style you like. You put it on your face to keep it warm, or you can stick it on your head if you prefer."

"But does it *meow?*" the waiter asked, remembering something he had read about cats.

"I haven't heard it meow, but it might if you hold it to your ear long enough," Flo said, trying to sound convincing.

"Really?" the waiter said putting it against his large lobes. "I can't hear anything?"

"Give it time," Flo said trying to think of something else to say to persuade the waiter to swap the beard for some of his delicious treats.

"How much time?" the waiter asked getting impatient. "I couldn't have it growling or hissing at any customers," he insisted, as Flo told him how her father had seen a beard on the face of a bus driver when he had visited Planet Earth. He had identified it with his naming device and had later grown his own beards from strands of hair he found in a field.

"I can imagine!" the waiter exclaimed, stroking the beard again. "Sorry … but I would have considered a cat. And anyway, I couldn't risk hairs falling into the food."

"Well, I have something else that you'll love," Flo told the waiter, stuffing *Hector's Beards* back in the box and lifting the *Paper with Flavour* onto her table.

"*Paper?*" the waiter said looking disinterestedly at the bundle of sheets. "Why would I want paper?"

"For writing menus, of course," Flo said confidently. "Record your favourite recipes, advertise, make posters for the Crater Café …"

"What's the point?" the waiter sighed wearily. "Hardly anyone comes. I was surprised to see *you*. Everyone's so scared they'll get hit by a flying rock."

"That *is* the point," Flo said in her most persuasive voice. "Write letters inviting everyone. Offer them an incentive like a free drink, buy one get one free, that kind of thing, and say there's not been a meteorite hit for ages."

"Are you crazy?" the waiter then laughed. "How would I post them? Everyone uses space mail these days. One press of a button and it's zapped through the Milky Way. Paper's a thing of the past."

"But it's not *any* old paper," Flo insisted, scrunching a strip of the paper into a ball and popping it into her mouth. "This is *Paper with Flavour*. "It's the most delicious tasting paper in the Universe."

"Really?" the waiter said in astonishment.

"Go on … try a piece," Flo said, tearing off a long, thin strip and handing it to the waiter. "You won't be disappointed."

"*Paper with Flavour?*" the waiter grinned, sliding it between his two front fangs.

"I like it!" he laughed, rolling it back and forth along his big fat tongue.

"Don't swallow it though," Flo warned him when he looked like he was about to. "It'll clog you up."

"So what do I do with it?" the waiter asked, spitting the soggy paper ball into his large purple hand when all the flavour had been sucked out.

"That's entirely up to you!" Flo grinned giving him the bundle of *Paper with Flavour* and reaching for the menu.

"Go on then," the waiter said taking out his notepad and pencil. "It's been ages since my taste buds experienced anything quite so ... so ... *unusual*. What would you like?"

"A bit of everything," Flo smiled. "Then I'll decide."

The asteroid meringues were lovely to start with; crunchy on the outside and chewy in the middle just like meringues should be. But when Flo's teeth stuck together she knew they were too chewy.

"Use this," the waiter said giving her some glue remover and it was some time before she could open her mouth again to try the nippy cinnamon sauce. That was even less palatable than the meringues. One lick and Flo's mouth was on fire.

"Nippy?" she gasped when she could eventually speak. "That stuff's a health hazard."

"Sorry!" the waiter apologised again, putting down his fire extinguisher when Flo looked like she had recovered. "It must be an acquired taste."

"I would rather not acquire it," Flo insisted, taking a spoonful of the comet surprise. But she was unprepared for the type of surprise it gave her. She started to bark … just little yelps at first but then a raging howl that made her jump out of her chair in fright.

"I can't apologise enough," the waiter said covering his ears. "That was the loudest one I've ever heard."

"It's okay," Flo said getting back on her chair. "Your recipe just needs some work."

"Any suggestions?" the waiter asked, handing her a free drink.

"I'll send you a space mail," Flo grinned, watching the ice cream bubble in the heat of the Sun. When she put it to her lips each mouthful was hotter and more wonderful than the one before.

"This is the one," she smiled to the waiter after guzzling the last sip.

"It's our speciality," the waiter said proudly, filling Flo's two flasks to the brim and telling her to come back if she ever got a cat.

Flo was delighted. She had traded one of her parents' weird inventions for a superb ingredient for the Perfect Pudding and not only that, she had an extra flask for them all to enjoy in the spaceship. Maybe trading the inventions wouldn't be so difficult after all. She wasted no time speeding home. Time was ticking, and she still had 220 million miles to go before she could reveal her ultimate cosmic experience.

4

The Second Ingredient

"Quick!" Hugo yelled, grabbing a flask from his sister's hands and running out of the space pod parking zone.

Flo ran after him and stared in horror. Her mother's arm had lost another few inches and her father's extra sensitive nose at the top of his head was gone. Hugo opened the flask of hot ice cream and started feeding it first to his mother, then to his father.

"Mind your manners and use a spoon, dear," Jemima said weakly, watching her son cup the white liquid in his hand.

"I was hoping it would grow back here and not on my bottom," Hector smiled when another nose shot out of his head. "It happened to my friend you know. A big nose popped out of his underside and he never sat down again."

"You have some strange friends," Jemima smiled, watching her arm sprout from the elbow.

"They're even stranger now," Hector grinned, smacking his lips.

"This is heavenly," Jemima drooled, taking the spoon off Hugo and shoving the hot ice cream into her hungry mouth.

"Fantastic," Hector agreed thrusting it down his throat. "And the waiter liked the *Paper with Flavour*?" he smiled when he had finished guzzling and Flo told them all about The Crater Café.

"He didn't swallow it though, did he?" Jemima said, recalling the time she had gulped it down and was so clogged up she wasn't right for ages.

"No, he didn't swallow it," Flo assured her.

"Pancakes?" Hugo smiled approvingly when his sister revealed her second ingredient for the Perfect Pudding as they blasted towards Planet Venus. It didn't come as too much of a surprise. He knew Flo adored pancakes.

"The secret of a first-class pancake is in the fold," she would say to anyone who came into the kitchen while she was making them. "If the fold isn't right the stuffing escapes and leaves a sticky mess all over the pan. If there's too much stuffing then even the best fold won't keep it in."

Flo's best ever pancake filling was melted toffee and jelly, but her spicy fillings were sensational too. Tough pancakes were essential for exercising their teeth, and since food in the spaceship was rationed they had all noticed wear and tear on their molars. The idea for squashed pancakes happened when Flo had dropped one on the floor and Hector had trodden on it.

"You can't eat that one," Jemima said in disgust when Hector peeled it off the floor and ate it.

"It's just a waste," Hector insisted, ignoring his wife.

"Volcano-smoked pancakes actually," Flo said when Hugo insisted on more details about the second ingredient for the Perfect Pudding.

"Do they explode?" he asked excitedly, whipping out his sketch pad.

"I don't think so!" Flo laughed, searching the Space Web for the description.

"That's too bad!" Hugo sighed. "It would have made a great advertising slogan. Just imagine, *Let the taste explode on your tongue*, or *Experience the explosion of flavours.* You know ... that sort of thing. What *do* volcano-smoked pancakes do then?" he said looking at their description.

"It says that volcano-smoked pancakes are cooked on a jet of volcanic gas by Val the volcanologist on Planet Venus," Flo read out, "They are the most flavoursome pancakes in the Solar System."

"And what shape are they?" Hugo asked, getting busy with his pencil.

"Round by the looks of it," Flo said, printing off a map and directions to the volcano-smoked pancakes.

"Too bad," Hugo groaned, "But we can soon fix that. Got any pictures?"

"Loads," Flo said, showing him a good one of Val the volcanologist with a volcano-smoked pancake balanced on her spatula.

"So pancakes (not round) with hot ice cream," Hugo said, turning his design pad to study his sketches from every angle. "The contrast of smooth ice cream with the crispness of a pancake will be interesting."

"I was thinking more of a soft, spongy pancake," Flo said, watching her brother sketch some more.

"I'll consider it!" Hugo smiled.

"Watch it!" Flo grinned. "You stick with the design and advertising and I'll deal with the cooking."

"You could roll up the side of the pancake and pour the hot ice cream inside," Hugo said when the idea popped into his head. "But the side might collapse and the ice cream spill all over the plate."

"Or... I could leave the pancake flat and drizzle the hot ice cream around it," Flo muttered switching off her computer.

"But you can't skimp on the design of the Perfect Pudding!" Hugo exclaimed at the suggestion she might. "How about rolling the pancake into a tube, filling it with hot ice cream and folding the ends?"

Flo looked at her brother and smiled. He *was* good ... and only sometimes annoying.

"By the way have you thought about giving away free samples of the Perfect Pudding at the Food and Fun Fest?" Hugo said closing his sketch pad for the night.

"Free?" Flo exclaimed, appalled by the suggestion. "That's your worst idea *yet*."

"Why?" Hugo said. "Just think ... If you give the customers a little taste of the pudding and they like it, they'll come back for more."

"It's too risky," Flo said diving into bed. "We'll have more chance of getting what we need and continuing with our space travels if the taste of the Perfect Pudding is a complete surprise."

"Not necessarily," Hugo said, pondering his research into "advertising that worked".

"If I hadn't studied my maps I would have been convinced there was nothing to see on Venus," Flo said, staring at the pale yellow globe that filled the spaceship window.

"That's because it's covered by a thick blanket of cloud that hides its surface from view," Hector explained trying to catch the crumbs falling from Flo's breakfast cracker.

"You could peek through the cloud layer with my radar telescope," Jemima said, savouring a big crumb that she had spotted under Hugo's chair.

But Flo didn't have time for that. After deliberately dropping more crumbs than usual she was in the space pod with two of Jemima's inventions getting ready for take-off. Revived by the hot ice cream, Hector had worked late into the night toughening up the pod's bodywork and fitting an extra thick heat shield. Flo had worked late herself, studying the directions to the volcano-smoked pancakes and familiarising herself with the Venusian landscape. When she zoomed out of the exit hatch the brightness was blinding and it was difficult to focus on the cloud layer. Only when the *Wingo* explained that clouds reflected sunlight and trapped heat did Flo understand why Venus was the brightest and hottest planet in the Solar System. The *Wingo* had been a late birthday present from her parents, and the little computer was bursting at the seams with fascinating facts about planets for her to listen to as she flew.

As if the light bouncing off the clouds wasn't challenging enough, as Flo flew closer to the pale yellow globe she realised the clouds were racing around Venus at top speed. Somehow she had to get through them. She looked for a way in, but the clouds were thick and spinning so rapidly that even if there was a gap she couldn't see it. There was nothing else for it. With a glance over her shoulder at her spaceship she flew in.

Visibility flashed "zero" on the space pod's alarm as Flo was swept along in the thick clouds. Faster and faster she went as winds beat the pod's wings and long, sleek tail. Then, when she saw that the protective outer heat shield was starting to curl up at the edges and the space pod's nose was pointing down instead of up, she wondered if she would ever taste a pancake again. The cloud composition dial was pointing to "acid". One kilometre, two kilometres ... further and further she flew through the scorching clouds. She was starting to think Venus might not be a planet at all but a massive ball of cloud, when she plunged into the masked world.

5

Volcano-smoked Pancakes

Venus had been completely shaped by volcanoes. Flat plains were covered in lava flows and craters filled to the brim with molten rock. Flo studied her directions. *"Follow the zig-zag road of lava rocks to the Pancake Dome on the lowland plains,"* it had said on the Space Web and just as she spotted it her satellite navigation system reacted to the heat and packed in.

The Pancake Dome was a volcanic structure, slightly bowl-shaped with a flat top and central vent, where thick lava had once flowed out and set … like a pancake in a pan. It was the name "Pancake Dome" that had inspired Val the volcanologist to cook her pancakes there in the first place.

"Come and get your volcano-smoked pancakes," she called to Flo when she saw her watching. "The secret's in the gas," she smiled flipping a triple-deluxe volcano-smoked pancake with her spatula. "It's the best cooking spot I've ever found. Would you like one?"

But Flo knew that everything depended on one thing.

"Have you ever fancied watching *Smelly-Vision*?" she asked Val, trying to make it sound like the best idea ever.

"Watching *what*?" Val said staring at her with the contraption.

"*Smelly-Vision*," Flo repeated in her most persuasive voice, "Just imagine ... you can cook your pancakes on the Dome and it will be possible to smell them all over the Milky Way."

"Now, that *would* be good for business," Val smiled, watching Flo switch it on. "How does it work exactly?"

"My mother invented it," Flo said proudly. "Electronic signals are turned into smells instead of the usual pictures and sounds. It adds a whole new dimension to Space TV."

"Okay, I'll try it," Val said putting down her spatula. "Viewers will be able to watch me whipping up a pancake and sniff it at the same time. I'll be famous!"

"Yes, it really is amazing!" Flo laughed, bowled over by Val's reaction to her mother's invention. "The smell blasts out of this tube."

Val took the tube between her long blue fingers and put it to her nose.

"That's disgusting!" she yelled when Flo tuned the TV in. "I have never, ever, in all my life smelt anything so revolting. In fact, I think I'm going to be sick."

"I'm so sorry," Flo apologised when she saw what film was showing on the screen. "I had absolutely no idea *The Alien with a Hundred Stinky Feet and Bad Breath* was on again."

"It's okay," Val said recovering from the shock. "Maybe *Smelly-Vision's* not such a great idea after all."

"What about *Tasty-Vision* then?" Flo suggested when Val got back to her cooking. "It's much better than *Smelly-*

Vision. My mother is an expert in taste-sensitive signals, and because of all her hard work it is now possible to *taste* what is on television."

"Does that include stinky feet?" Val said looking suspiciously at the invention.

"That's entirely up to you," Flo said running her thick blubbery tongue across the screen. "With *Tasty-Vision* you can see exactly what you're licking."

"Do you mean I can cook a pancake here on the Dome and it will be possible to taste it without even coming?" Val asked, not sure if she liked that idea at all.

"You can taste it, but you can't eat it," Flo clarified. "If you like the taste you can come and get some. That will be even better for business."

"Okay, I'll try it," Val said putting down her spatula again. "But I want to see what I'm licking this time. No surprises."

"No problem," Flo smiled tuning it in. "What about this?"

Val looked at the screen and smiled approvingly. It was her favourite programme *Cook with Max* and Max was whipping up his delicious-looking custard. She began to slide her tongue back and forth across the screen.

"This custard is a bit lumpy," she said enjoying the unusual sensation. "And it has the most unusual flavour."

Flo looked at the screen but it was too late to do anything. The signal was poor and the channel had changed.

"Ahhhhh," Val screamed when she saw the huge mouth full of sharp teeth coming in her direction.

Flo could only apologise again. "I'm so sorry," she said holding Val's arm to steady her. "The channel does occasionally change by itself and if I had known there was a documentary on about hungry crocodiles on Planet Earth I would never have taken the chance."

"Okay," Val said when she could eventually speak. "Your mother needs to sort out the channel-changing thing and until then I'm not interested. In fact, I've never been less interested in anything in all my years on the Dome. My nose hasn't recovered and my taste buds are still numb."

Flo was desperate as she watched Val get back to her cooking. It was torture; to be so close to something so delicious, yet be denied it for the Perfect Pudding.

"Have you got *anything* of interest in your box?" Val then said when she saw that Flo hadn't gone. "I haven't had a customer for a while and I would have liked your opinion about my new triple-deluxe volcano-smoked pancake."

"I have nothing else," Flo told her, opening the box of inventions and checking every corner.

"Actually ... that's a nice space pod you've got there," Val then said eyeing up Flo's pod and pointing over to it with her dripping spatula.

"Sorry, you can't have that," Flo said surprised by Val's suggestion.

"I didn't mean to keep," Val grinned tossing her pancakes. "I meant to try. It's been ages since I took to the skies, and all this volcanic gas is starting to affect my skin flaps."

"Look ... there are no customers at the moment," Val said, sensing Flo's uncertainty. "I haven't had a break for the longest time. How would you like it ... being stuck here day in and day out, making pancakes. Don't get me wrong, I love making pancakes, but everyone needs a change now and again. And, anyway ... I'll make it worth your while."

"How?" Flo said getting interested.

"Well ... You let me fly your pod, and I'll let you try the new triple-deluxe volcano-smoked pancake," Val told her. "You can have anything else you want after that."

Without waiting for a reply Val stripped off her apron and ran to the pod, passing her spatula to Flo en route.

"Can you cook?" she yelled from the flying seat. "Just keep scooping in the batter and watch things don't get too hot."

Flo stared in disbelief at the spatula in her green hand. Val couldn't be serious. But of course she was.

Her first customers were a couple of Martians, chatty and friendly enough and happy to wait a bit longer than usual for Flo to get the hang of cooking at the Dome. By the time the family from Ganymede came to get their four extra large pancakes to go she could have been doing it for years. But even so she was relieved to see the pod zooming out of the clouds.

"That was brilliant!" Val smiled tying her apron strings, "Very nippy and great steering. I feel totally re-energised. Thank you."

"No problem!" Flo said handing back the spatula. "The Martians left you a bag of comet crumbles and the family from Ganymede said they'll hand in a large rock cake next time they're passing."

"And you believed them?" Val huffed stuffing a crumble into her hungriest mouth. "They said that the last time. By the way, did you taste a pancake?"

"No," Flo lied.

She had made three extra pancakes — by accident of course — and devoured them whole. They exceeded all her expectations. As she wiped the sweet sticky trickles from her bumpy chin she knew that volcano-smoked pancakes would be a sensational addition to the Perfect Pudding and would improve her family's chance of space travel no end for another year.

Val watched as Flo chomped on the new triple-deluxe volcano-smoked pancake.

"So?" she said, waiting for Flo to say something.

"Awesome!" Flo smiled, holding out her empty tub for Val to fill with her special pancake mix.

With a can of volcano-smoked gas stuffed securely behind her seat and the tub filled to the brim, Flo had everything she had come for. From the safety of her pod she watched red lava burst out of a large shield volcano just below the horizon. Large rocks hurled out of the gaping vent, and then, as it began to settle, a flash of lightning illuminated the sky. As she flew towards the sky she gave the thumbs up to Val who was busy as ever with her spatula. Then, with a final look at the twists and turns of the zig-zag road, she flew up into the thick clouds leaving the veiled planet behind her.

But she wouldn't have been quite so jubilant had she known her parents were devouring the first ingredient for her Perfect Pudding.

6

The First Ingredient is Snaffled

The moment the pod touched down on the floor of the spaceship Flo knew something was wrong. Hugo was wiping tears from his eye.

"I tried to stop them," he sniffed at the door of the pod, "But by the time I saw what was going on, it was too late."

"What are you talking about?" Flo said, stepping down and reaching out her hand to comfort him.

"The hot ice cream …" Hugo told her. "It's gone!"

"You'll never guess what happened!" Hector then exclaimed, rushing over to the pod and throwing his longest arm around his daughter. "While you were away we found another, *bigger* flask of hot ice cream under your bed."

"Did you really?" Flo said, hiding her distress.

"Did you forget about it, dear?" Jemima said dashing over to the pod and giving her a big hug.

"I was keeping it for emergencies," Flo lied.

"That's what I said!" Hector smiled. "And when I saw your mother's chin start to curl up at the end, I knew you would want her to have some."

"Yes, dear, it was so thoughtful of you," Jemima smiled. "I would have been devastated every time I looked in the mirror."

"But did you have to finish it?" Flo said noticing that her father was looking more energised than ever. "There's nothing wrong with *your* chin."

"That's true," Hector grinned, admiring his handsome cone-shaped chin in the space pod's wing mirror. "But I was famished. I was all over the spaceship on my hands and knees looking for crumbs. You can imagine how I felt when I saw the flask; the beautiful, big flask of delicious hot ice cream under your bed."

"I *can* imagine," Flo said, devastated at the loss of her precious ingredient.

"I just couldn't resist," Hector admitted. "And before I knew it I had opened it up and the rest ... well, the rest is history."

"That's when I caught them," Hugo mumbled, trying to hide his distress. "I tried to stop it happening, but I was so traumatised when I saw them lying on their backs pouring your precious ingredient down their throats that I couldn't even speak."

"It's okay," Flo said, trying to assure her brother he had done his best.

"So they didn't even offer you a drop?" Flo asked Hugo when he came to her bedroom for their late-night blether.

"Well, they did actually," Hugo recalled, sinking into a cushion. "But it was right at the bottom of the flask where Dad's tongue had been flicking non-stop."

"Say no more!" Flo groaned at the thought.

"This is spectacular!" Hugo smiled, wolfing down a volcano-smoked pancake.

Flo had brought one back for them all to share, but under the circumstances had decided her brother could have it all.

"So Val wasn't convinced about the *Smelly- and Tasty-Visions*?" he asked, when Flo told him all about her visit to Planet Venus.

"She says they have potential!" Flo said, studying the maps of the Milky Way Galaxy on her computer.

They had stopped watching *Smelly- and Tasty-Vision* themselves. It was just too cruel to be able to smell and taste a delicious flavour but not be able to actually eat anything and fill your belly.

"If we increase our speed we might have time to visit one more planet after Mars," Flo muttered, thinking out loud and doing some calculations. "We'll be at Earth in the morning, Mars a few days after that, and if we blast on all engines we might even make it to Jupiter before the Food and Fun Fest."

"You mean you're still thinking about making the Perfect Pudding?" Hugo said polishing off the last bite of the scrumptious pancake and sitting down beside her at the computer.

"I may have to improvise," Flo told him, savouring every word in the latest newsletter from Star Excel, the top space college in the Milky Way, "But even top chefs have to do that!"

Everyone in Flo's family knew that Star Excel was where Flo dreamed of going to one day, if she was ever lucky enough to get a place there. There were lots of colleges where you could study cooking, but none exceeded Star Excel in reputation. That was where you were guaranteed to be trained by the best chefs in the Universe and Flo wanted nothing less.

"I'm glad you've not been put off by the hot ice cream," Hugo said opening up his drawing pad. "I've got some ideas I want to run past you."

Flo looked at his pictures of rolled-up pancakes. They were excellent.

"Of course, the hot ice cream will have to come out now," he said showing her some more, "But I can adapt and change my designs depending on what ingredients you get. Oh yes, I've been thinking ... we'll need to work on the snappy line."

"The snappy *what*?" Flo said, starting her research into ingredients on Planet Earth.

"A slogan," Hugo explained. "We need to sum up the Perfect Pudding in one snappy line."

"Why do we have to do *that*?" Flo asked, reading her computer screen.

"It's a powerful advertising tool," Hugo said recalling what he had read about it on the Space Web. "We need to think of a short sentence that will make The Perfect Pudding irresistible to the customer. Here's a couple I've thought up already. What about *The Perfect Pudding — the best pudding in the Universe*?"

"It's good!," Flo smiled. "We have to be confident to make it convincing."

"Or ... *The Perfect Pudding — Your taste buds deserve it.*"

"They're both good!" Flo grinned, getting back to her research.

"What are *those*?" Hugo exclaimed, staring at the oval, yellowish-red fruits Flo was looking at on the computer.

"Mangoes," Flo said, reading their name and description.

"They're a bit big to sit on a pancake!" Hugo laughed grabbing his pencil and sketch pad. "Maybe you could cut them up."

"I hope so," Flo grinned, deciding their sweet taste and buttery texture would be ideal for the Perfect Pudding.

"Bananas!" Hugo laughed when he saw their picture. He recognised them from his father's description. They had been the origin of *Paper with Flavour*. His grandfather had brought one back from his trip to Planet Earth and reproduced the flavour in his laboratory.

"This star apple fruit looks amazing!" Flo said, turning her screen towards Hugo, who was busy sketching alternatives to the rolled pancake, including a triangular-shaped pancake and a diamond pancake.

"The purple colour's interesting," he smiled looking up from his pad, "Nothing wishy-washy about it."

"You'll love this bit," Flo said, searching for another picture. "When you slice them open there's a star pattern inside."

"So ... volcano-smoked pancakes with mango and banana and a slice of star apple fruit," Hugo said thinking out loud. "The design possibilities are endless."

"But it needs a sauce," Flo sighed, yanking her recipe books off the shelf. "The ice cream would have been perfect."

"Got it!" she eventually said after studying pages and pages of puddings. "I'll make a purée!"

"A what?" Hugo said, watching Flo switch off her computer and dive into bed.

"An exotic rainforest purée," she yawned, closing her eye.

"How do you do that?" Hugo asked, desperate for details.

"Just wait and see," Flo smiled. "But there's one thing you must promise me before I head off to Planet Earth …"

"Yes?" Hugo said, getting back to work on advertising slogans.

"If you see anyone's tongue flicking anywhere near the big locked cupboard at the back of the kitchen where I've decided to hide Val's special pancake mix and can of volcano-smoked gas, cut it off, or it will be the end of the Perfect Pudding and our space travels."

"With pleasure!" Hugo laughed.

7

Rainforest Fruit

Flo threw open her bedroom curtains and stared in awe at the brilliant blue sphere. The swirling white clouds didn't hide this planet's surface like the Venusian clouds had. Patches of green and brown stood out like coloured beads within the blue crown. Planet Earth was a giant jigsaw where the pieces fitted together perfectly. It even had a grey and dimpled moon.

"Earth looks blue because of water," Hector explained when he looked in Flo's bedroom and saw her staring out the window.

"They're lucky to have it!" Jemima smiled, sitting down on her daughter's bed clutching a cup of stewed space plant leaves. "They can drink it, swim in it, and even wash their socks in it."

"Who are *they*?" Flo asked, her eye still fixed on the view.

"Earthlings, of course," Jemima smiled, taking a gulp of her tea. "I think I saw one last time I was here, but I can't be sure."

"What was it like?" Flo asked, intrigued. She had been so busy researching ingredients on Earth; she hadn't given any thought to its inhabitants.

"It was swinging from a tree," Jemima remembered from her sighting of the strange-looking creature with the long tail.

"That wasn't an *Earthling*, dear," Hector perked up after his second cup of their tasteless morning brew.

"How do you know?" Jemima retorted, indignant at her husband's know-it-all attitude.

"Because Earthlings have *beards* and drive a *bus*," Hector said with confidence.

"I saw something slide across the ground, and something else flying ... without an engine," Jemima smiled smugly.

"No! Really?" Flo gasped. She couldn't wait to see that!

"I adored my visit to Earth," Jemima sighed, thinking back to the beautiful Amazon Rainforest.

"It's home to more than half of the planet's animal and plant species," she could still recall her father telling her.

And that was why Flo had decided the rainforest was where she would find her next ingredient for the Perfect Pudding. She wasted no time jetting off in the space pod with yet another box of her parents' inventions. The *Smelly-and Tasty-Visions had* been useless but she was more optimistic about *Hector's Paint* and the *Zapa-Snapa*. With her navigational device pre-set to take her there, all she had to do was sit back and enjoy the ride. And after discovering that the jigsaw was even more beautiful the closer she got to it, she flew through the rainforest canopy to the forest floor.

Flo had often heard her mother describing the rainforest. It had been interesting to hear her talk about the huge umbrella of branches blocking out the Sun from the forest floor, and she had spoken about creatures living in the different layers of the forest. But it was the noise of the rainforest that *really* surprised her. Jemima had mentioned the quacking and croaking, but there were squawks and squeals high up in the trees, and crunching and rustling all around her.

She hoped to spot an Earthling, but wasn't sure if she would recognise one even if she did. What she didn't know was that an Earthling had already spotted *her*. Her name was Elena and she had noticed the strange creature with its box while picking lipstick tree fruit to dye the bags she made from palm tree fibre. *Possibly a relative of the sloth*, Elena thought. She was used to seeing the animals hanging out in the huge trees. Sloths were harmless so she decided it was probably safe to approach the sloth-like animal.

When Flo saw the strange, one-nosed creature coming her way she darted behind a tree.

"Do you fly without an engine or slide along the ground?" was all she could think to say when she plucked up the courage to face it.

Elena screamed. She had never heard a sloth *talk*.

"Or perhaps you swing from a tree?" Flo tried again, realising that she had upset the creature.

Elena started to run but tripped over a tree root and fell down.

"Let me help you," Flo said reaching out her hand.

Elena stared at the slimy green hand with the bony fingers and then looked at Flo. "What *are* you?" she said getting to her feet but declining the offer of the hand.

"What am *I*?" Flo laughed at the absurd question. "What are *you*?"

"I'm a girl, of course," Elena grinned. She decided that a talking sloth was *very* strange, but she had always kept an open mind to the possibility of new species in the rainforest.

"Is that a beard on your head?" Flo then asked, pointing to Elena's flowing brown locks.

"A *beard*?" Elena repeated in bewilderment. The sloth-like animal said the most bizarre things.

"My grandfather has a long bushy beard and my grandmother has a few stray whiskers but that's about it for beards in our family," she giggled, starting to enjoy the amusing company of the talking sloth … even if it had just insulted her best feature.

"Where's your bus?" Flo asked, looking around for a large vehicle like the one her father had described to her.

"I don't know much about buses!" Elena laughed, "But I can paddle a canoe faster than most adults ... and I can hunt and fish."

Flo liked the girl, and she liked her even more when Elena picked a mango from a tree, cut it open and handed her a slice. She was so tempted to just take it. But that wouldn't have been fair.

"Could I interest you in some paint?" she asked, lifting a pot from her box.

"*Paint*?" Elena said in surprise. "Why would I want paint?"

"Let me show you," Flo offered, wrenching the lid off with the claw on her left wrist and dabbing some on Elena's bag.

"Not bad," Elena smiled. "It's an unusual colour."

"That's because it's a *new* colour," Flo explained confidently. "My father made it. He was bored with all the usual blue, red and greens. It's a cross between tangerine and olive."

"Sorry, I'm not really interested in paint," Elena said. "I have enough colours to choose from in the rainforest and I like to make my own shades."

"What about a *Zapa-Snapa* then?" Flo suggested, taking it out of her box.

"A zapa *what*?" Elena said looking at the strange gadget.

"I'll show you," Flo offered walking to a tree and zapping one of the fruits.

"It's gone!" Elena said in surprise, looking at where the mango had been.

"It's still there," Flo assured her.

"That's impossible," Elena laughed, feeling the fruit she couldn't see. "Are you playing tricks on me?"

"Not at all," Flo insisted zapping her bag.

"Did your father make that as well?" she asked when she had recovered from the shock of her bag disappearing too.

"Oh yes," Flo smiled proudly. "He's been working on invisibility for some time, but unfortunately he's still not got it quite right."

"That's fine!" Elena said looking at the mango and her bag that had reappeared. "I don't want to lose my bag, and I would if I couldn't see it!"

"So, would you like one?" Flo asked, handing Elena the *Zapa-Snapa*.

"I would love one!" Elena laughed zapping her finger. "I'll have lots of fun with this!"

Flo picked a mango and bit into the hard skin.

"Let me help you!" Elena giggled, taking it from her and slicing it open with the knife she carried for cutting the palm tree fibre.

When Flo tasted the sweet, juicy fruit with the delicious buttery texture she knew it was exactly what she wanted for her rainforest purée. Then when she spotted a bunch of bananas hanging from the plant with the massive leaves she knew the cocktail of flavours would be unbeatable.

It was easy to forget about time with so many tempting rainforest fruits to choose from, but she was determined to stick to her plan.

"Can you point me in the direction of the star apple tree?" she asked Elena, when she said she had to get back to her family.

Flo recognised the tree immediately; the glossy, green leaves with the shimmering gold underside, and the round, purple-skinned fruits. But she had to be sure. She picked a fruit and cut it open. There was no mistaking the star-shaped pattern in the red pulp. She scooped the soft flesh with her fingers and thrust it greedily into her mouth. It was sensational; sweet, yet not too sweet, and juicier than she imagined anything could be. It even had an unusual sweet-scented smell. It would be a *huge* hit at the Food and Fun Fest and superb for the Perfect Pudding.

She worked quickly, filling her crate, stacking star apple fruit, mangoes, and bananas in rows, careful not to waste any space. Then, when she was sure she had everything she needed for her masterpiece she was off in her space pod, through the gap in the trees where a giant kapok tree had once stood before being struck down by a bolt of lightning. During the day the Sun flowed through the hole shining a bright beam of light onto the forest floor, but now the sky was beginning to darken.

With her navigational device set to take her home, she watched the jigsaw unfold below her; the trees and rivers, hills and flatlands dotted with every colour of the rainbow. It was only when they were tiny dots below her that she looked up towards the flashing orange lights in the sky, with a smile on her face as wide as a rainforest banana. But she wouldn't have been smiling quite so widely had she known her father's nose was within sniffing range of the pancake mix and volcano-smoked gas.

8

The Crunchy Topping

"There's something in there and I want it!" Hector bawled, trying to push his nose even further through the hole he had drilled in the big locked cupboard at the back of the kitchen.

"You wouldn't keep food from us, dear, would you?" Jemima asked her daughter when she raced into the kitchen to see what all the shouting was about.

"There's no chance of that!" Flo exclaimed, staring horrified at her father with his longest nose dangerously close to her treasured ingredient. In a split second she decided what to do.

"Anyone like a banana?" she yelled, opening up the crate and pulling out a bunch.

"Bananas!" Jemima cried excitedly, abandoning her husband at the cupboard and grabbing them from Flo's hand.

That was when Hector got so excited at the sound of his wife munching and slobbering he yanked his nose out of the hole stripping off the skin. His nose was pink instead of green but the bananas were so delicious he didn't feel the pain, and when they had scoffed the lot he was back at the cupboard again.

"There is *definitely* something in there," he insisted sticking his nose back in the hole, "And I'm going to get it!"

"It's your imagination," Hugo told him opening the cupboard door wide so his father could see inside.

Hector stared disbelievingly at the empty shelves. The bananas had been the perfect distraction. While his parents were scoffing them one by one, Hugo had managed to slip the pancake mix and volcano-smoked gas out of the kitchen.

"I was so sure I could smell something fantastic in there," Hector said suspiciously, running his long, bony finger along the cupboard shelves, inspecting them for crumbs, but there wasn't even a trace.

Storing the ingredients for the Perfect Pudding had become a serious problem for Flo.

"Where do you think we should hide them?" she asked her brother when their parents had gone to bed, and he came to her room to apologise for not cutting Hector's tongue off like he had promised.

"Somewhere Dad's noses can't reach," Hugo said, looking at the ingredients under his sister's bed.

That was the problem with their father having three noses pointing in different directions. They both knew that no matter where Flo hid the ingredients he would eventually sniff them out.

"There's only one thing to do," Flo decided switching on her computer, "I'll take them with me. Losing a whole bunch of bananas wasn't good, but losing any more would be the end of the rainforest purée, and losing the mango, the star fruit or the pancake mix would be the end of the Perfect Pudding."

"You did great at the blue planet!" Hugo smiled, lifting the lid off the crate to admire the latest ingredients. "Do these really have a star inside?" he asked, taking out a star apple fruit and handling it carefully.

"They do!" Flo smiled beginning to research ingredients on Planet Mars. "I'll use the mango and the banana and a little of that for the purée."

"Yes, but keep slices for the top of the pancake," Hugo said studying his designs.

"The purée shouldn't touch the pancake," Flo decided. "I want the flavours in the Perfect Pudding to remain quite distinct until they come together on the spoon."

"Rolling or folding the pancakes is definitely the best idea," Hugo mumbled deep in thought.

"Why's that then?" Flo said, studying a map of the Great Martian Canyons.

"Because if they get burnt they will be easier to hide," Hugo grinned.

"Burnt?" Flo exclaimed, appalled by the suggestion.

"Just in case!" Hugo laughed.

"How's the snappy line going?" Flo asked watching her brother draw in his sketch pad.

"Great!" Hugo smiled. "I'm now considering *Perfection: It's arrived. One taste and you're hooked*."

"That's great!" Flo nodded approvingly. "Are you still thinking about free samples?"

"I am," Hugo told her, "But only if we have to. Word of mouth is another powerful advertising tool, and once word gets out about how amazing the Perfect Pudding is, we might not have to give anything away. And ... as well as all of this, I'm also considering advertising on balloons," he said, holding up a picture of a big balloon with *Perfection: It's arrived!* printed on it.

"Balloons!" Flo said in surprise. "Do we have any?"

"Not exactly," Hugo sighed, "But do you remember *Hector's Inflatables*?"

"I'd rather not," Flo groaned, remembering the explosion and tiny pieces of green balloon that stuck like glue to everything they fell on."

"But we can deflate them before they explode," Hugo assured her, showing some more pictures of balloons with slogans.

"But what if we get the timing wrong?" Flo pointed out. "Our space travels will be doomed."

"You could be right," Hugo nodded, scanning his list of advertising ideas. "But I definitely think we should send out a space mail to everyone we know who goes to the Food and Fun Fest."

"Why's that then?" Flo said, printing off a map.

"To create mystery and intrigue around the Perfect Pudding," Hugo smiled, proud of his latest idea. "If we announce *The Perfect Pudding ... it's coming!* everyone will be tempted to taste it when they see it."

"Will they?" Flo asked curiously.

"Of course!" Hugo said with confidence. "It will make everyone *think* about what a *perfect* pudding could taste like even before they've seen it, and then when they *do* see it, they won't be able to resist finding out if they were right. By the way, how's your research going?"

"I'm looking for something irresistible to stuff the pancake with," Flo told him, scanning a description of Martian jelly. "I want something soft … something melt in the mouth."

"You don't want more soft," Hugo said reading the description. "The pudding needs *bite*."

"Bite?" Flo repeated in surprise.

"You know … *crunch*!" Hugo exclaimed. "The pudding needs crunch to contrast with the smoothness of the fruit. If all the ingredients are soft, anyone who likes a bit of bite in a dessert won't be interested."

"That's a point," Flo nodded approvingly; "The pudding has to appeal to as many customers as possible."

"Well ... how does this sound?" she asked, returning to the description of an ingredient she had read about earlier. "Martian marshmallows are not soft like your typical marshmallow. Martian marshmallows are creamy, sweet and surprisingly crunchy."

"Crunchy," Hugo repeated approvingly. "That's more like it. So ... where exactly do you get them?"

"That could be the challenge," Flo said, pointing to what looked like an enormous ragged scar stretched across Mars' equator. "But there're lots of landmarks on the way."

"The Valles Marineris Canyonlands," Hugo read from the map. "And who makes these marshmallows?"

"Him!" Flo grinned showing Hugo a picture on the computer of a big hefty Martian with a pink marshmallow wedged between his two front fangs sitting in a pink and white space pod.

"The Martian Marshmallow Maker!" Hugo laughed, drawing some marshmallows on top of the pancake designs. "That's original!"

Flo was now studying the Martian maps intently. From her bedroom window she had watched the radiant red disc swell from a tiny ruby into a magnificent red ball. Already she could make out some of the features on the Martian surface; strange looking lines and the massive scar. She would work all night to finalise her plans for getting the best crunchy topping for the Perfect Pudding.

9

Martian Marshmallows

Gazing out of the spaceship window Hector remembered *his* visit to the red planet when he was nine.

"I had to get back quickly," he recalled, chewing on a banana skin.

"Why?" Flo asked, deciding that banana skin was too bitter and opting for a dry cracker instead.

"Powerful winds blew rusty red dirt all over my space pod and my wipers failed," Hector said, thinking back to the frightening journey.

"How did you see?" Flo gasped, trying to imagine the terrible scene.

"I had to stick my hand out the window and clear the dust away with my jelly sandwich," Hector recalled, wrapping the banana skin around his fingers to stimulate growth. "A waste of a sandwich, but without it the consequences would have been fatal."

"It could have been worse, dear," Jemima said, munching on her banana skin before wrapping it around her toes that had shrunk in the night.

"How?" Hector asked thinking that most unlikely.

"It could have been a jelly and custard sandwich," she teased, remembering her husband's passion for that wicked combination.

"What's that?" Hugo asked at the sight of the strange shaped rock in orbit around the red planet.

"That's Deimos," Hector remembered. "Phobos, the other Martian moon, is over there," he said pointing out the window.

Flo studied the Martian moons through her telescope. She could see them both clearly now. They weren't like Earth's round moon; the Martian moons were potato-shaped chunks of rock. Phobos looked like someone had taken a huge bite out of it. Deimos was smoother, but that was possibly because its craters were filled to the brim with moon dust.

She had been up early, packing the pod with the ingredients for the Perfect Pudding. Leaving them was now totally out of the question since her father's fingers had shrivelled to his knuckles and he would soon be on the prowl again. But that hadn't stopped Hector getting up even earlier than his daughter to fit extra-strong wipers to the front windscreen of the pod and install an MPS.

"A Mars Positional System receiver," he said proudly when he saw his daughter studying the high-tech gadget. It had taken a lot of skill and effort for him to upgrade their navigational device but, remembering the powerful Martian winds, he had been determined to make Flo's visit to the red planet as safe as possible.

Flo had absolutely no time to get lost now that she was only 150 million miles away from the Food and Fun Fest. She had to get the amazing crunchy topping that would contrast with the smooth rainforest purée. Only *then* would she be satisfied that the Perfect Pudding was *perfect*. The red planet had exactly what she wanted and she had never felt so determined in her life as she loaded two of her parents' inventions, and all the ingredients for the Perfect Pudding, into the pod and flew out of the spaceship into the pink Martian sky.

She checked the MPS and flew east, close to the equator towards the elevated continent of Tharsis. Something in the past, possibly a Mars-quake had split the surface of the planet, lifting up the Tharsis region. Now like a large swelling it bulged out of the planet's surface. She flew further, over thousands of dry riverbeds while the *Wingo* explained that water had once flowed in volumes large enough to carve the face of the planet. On and on she flew until she came to a volcano so massive its nose poked through the pink clouds — Olympus Mons, the biggest volcano in the Solar System. But there was no time to stop for a better look. She was almost at the huge crack which split the surface of the planet. She had to get to the Martian Marshmallow Maker.

She flew into the Giant Canyon and along walls that had collapsed in gigantic landslides. She studied her map and began her descent. The Martian Marshmallow Maker's pink and white space pod was unmissable on the rocky canyon floor.

"Would you like to try a free sample?" the Martian Marshmallow Maker asked when he saw Flo eyeing up his delicious treats.

Flo nodded eagerly and popped a Martian marshmallow into her mouth. She began to chew. It was incredible; creamy and sweet and not surprisingly crunchy, because she knew that they were. She wanted them more than ever.

"I have exactly what you need for picking up all these crumbs," Flo said to the Martian Marshmallow Maker, lifting Hector's *Sucking and Sorting Hoover* out of her box and showing it to him.

"How rude!" the Martian Marshmallow Maker said, offended at the suggestion he was messy, which without a doubt he was.

"Sorry!" Flo said apologetically. She knew her choice of words had been careless, but with the delicious taste of marshmallow in her mouth she wasn't thinking straight.

"It recycles, so helps the environment," Flo explained, trying desperately to convince the Martian Marshmallow Maker that a *Sucking and Sorting Hoover* was a great thing to have.

"I'll take a look at it," the Martian Marshmallow Maker agreed, when his mallows were in the cooking pot and he had a moment to spare.

"These are the different compartments," Flo told him, drawing his attention to the little drawers at the front of the hoover. "The hoover sorts anything you programme it to separate, and instead of everything going into the same big bag, it spits all the bits into the correct drawers for recycling."

"Does that say '*toenails*?'" the Martian Marshmallow Maker asked, looking at the names on the drawers.

"It does indeed say toenails," Flo replied confidently.

"And what would *I* do with the toenails?" the Martian Marshmallow Maker asked with genuine interest.

"If you stick them all together just *imagine* what you could do with toenails," Flo said as convincingly as she could.

"I'm trying to, dear," the Martian Marshmallow Maker grinned. "I just hope you clean them first."

"And *those*?" he asked, pointing to a drawer that said '*crumbs*'. "What would I do with crumbs?"

"You could stick them all together and make a biscuit," Flo said wracking her brain for ideas.

"But is it hygienic, dear?" the Martian Marshmallow Maker said, turning his back on Flo and the invention. "I'm all for recycling and saving the environment, but this is going a bit too far."

Flo watched the Martian Marshmallow Maker at work. She had been unprepared for his questions; too busy thinking about the crunchy topping to rehearse how she would get it. She felt despair as the creamy, pink marshmallows tumbled out of the big cooking pot into the jar and the Martian Marshmallow Maker talked non-stop: strange stories about his ancestors who had made canals to transport water from melting polar ice caps on Mars, and how it had been a desperate last attempt. The climate had changed on the red planet and dried it up.

But she wasn't in any mood for stories. She had one more invention with her; one last chance to get her hands on the marshmallows of her dreams.

"I have something here that you'll love," she said reaching into her box and pulling out one of her mother's inventions.

The Martian Marshmallow Maker looked doubtfully at the thing in Flo's hand.

"It's an *Inflatable Spare Room with Clean Towels for Visitors*," she told him with all the enthusiasm she could muster.

"A *what?*" the Martian Marshmallow Maker said in amazement, as Flo pulled out a foot pump and began to inflate it.

"I've never seen anything so ridiculous in my life," the Martian Marshmallow Maker laughed as the inflatable room got bigger and bigger.

"They're great for visitors," Flo insisted, lying down on the bed to show the size. "We have several."

"Do you now!" The Martian Marshmallow Maker grinned. "Sorry, but I'm not interested in visitors unless they have something interesting to offer me, and this isn't one of them."

"What about the clean towels then?" Flo asked, desperately holding one up for him to see.

"I don't wash," the Martian Marshmallow Maker said getting back to work. "It's so dusty here, there's no point."

Flo loaded the *Sucking and Sorting Hoover* and the *Inflatable Spare Room with Clean Towels for Visitors* back into the box. It was time for her to go home. With tears in her eye she flew up and out of the largest and deepest canyon in the Solar System, but this time she was blind to the breathtaking scenery. She ploughed through the upper reaches of the atmosphere and disappeared like Martian water above the pink midday sky.

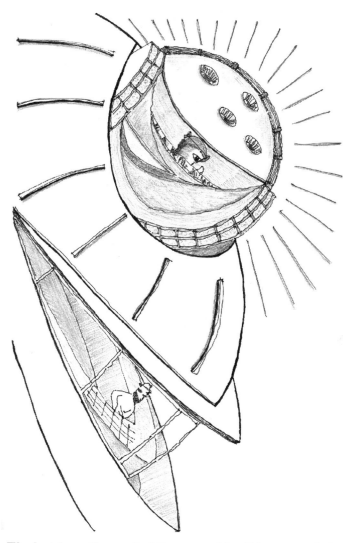

**The hatch on the roof of the spaceship slid open and she
stared down at the holey planet**

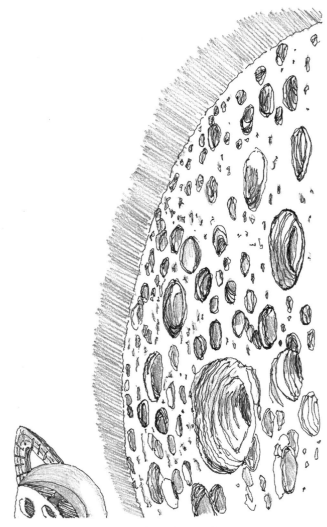

There were very few places that were not covered in craters

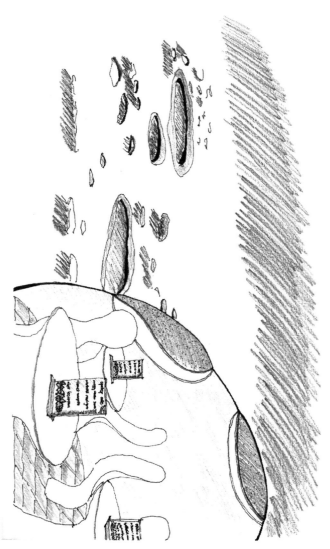

The Crater Café

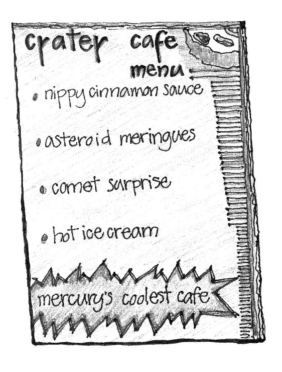

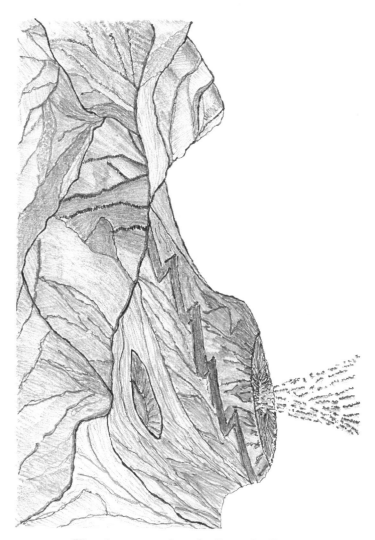

The zig-zag road to the Pancake Dome

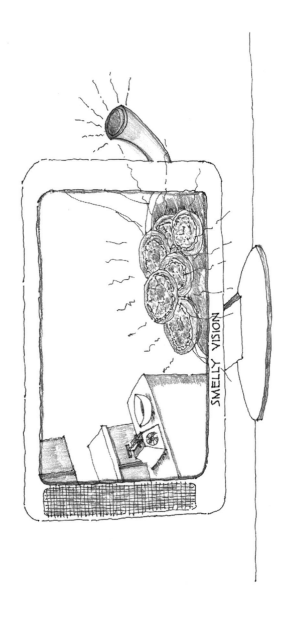

Hugo wolfs down a volcano-smoked pancake

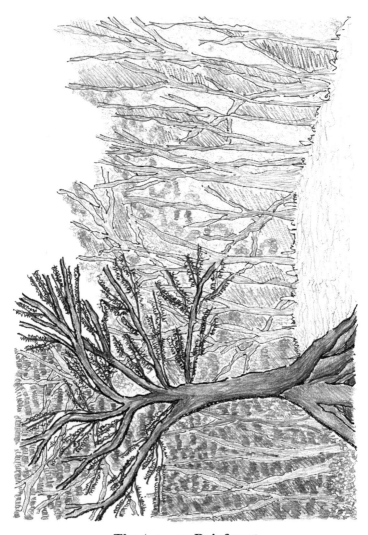

The Amazon Rainforest

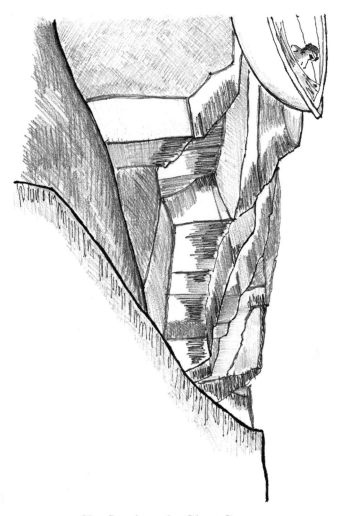

She flew into the Giant Canyon

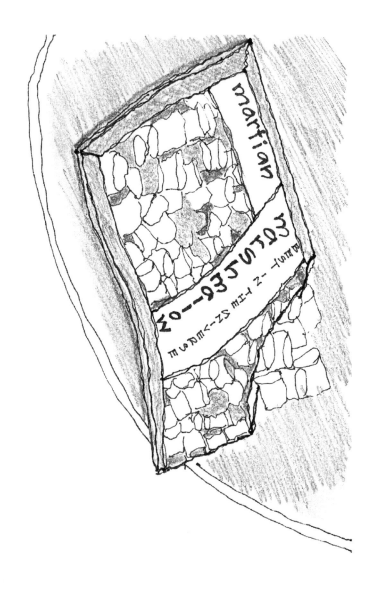

10

Syrupy Sprinkles

Hector, Jemima and Hugo knew from the devastated look on Flo's face that things had not gone according to plan.

"It's okay," Hector said when she stepped out of the pod. "We found a packet of crackers."

"Yes, it's a *big* packet!" Jemima smiled, trying her best to sound cheerful while hiding her hand that was dangling from a thin strip of skin.

"Let's celebrate your return," Hector suggested, leading everyone away from the space pod. "We'll have two crackers for dinner instead of one."

Hugo watched his sister chew her dry cracker. She was usually so full of stories on her return from the planets, but now she was silent. Hugo shared her disappointment. She had had an idea; a brilliant idea about making the ultimate cosmic experience using ingredients from across the Solar System, but either their parents had eaten, or were trying to eat, the ingredients, or she couldn't get them.

"We've still got volcano-smoked pancakes *and* rainforest fruits," he told her that evening when he went to her bedroom and found her staring vacantly out of the window.

"But it's not enough," Flo muttered, unable to hide her disappointment.

"I'll make a pudding," she said, still staring out the window, "It will be a *nice* pudding, but it won't be perfect."

"Does it *have* to be perfect?" Hugo asked, joining her at the window. "I mean, what *is* perfect?"

"It was to increase our chances of doing well at the Food and Fun Fest," Flo reminded him. "So we can travel the galaxies and do all the wonderful things we love to do as a family, without having to worry about running out of food supplies."

"I remember," Hugo said taking the telescope from his sister's hand and studying the skies. He had enjoyed designing the Perfect Pudding and working on the advertising just as much as she had enjoyed coming up with the recipe.

"We'll be at the Food and Fun Fest in the morning," Flo sighed despondently. She had already spotted the massive doughnut-shaped cluster of rocks flying in orbit between Mars and Jupiter.

"Yes, we'll be early," Hugo said, gazing at the rocks in the distance.

"Early?" Flo repeated, staring at him in surprise. "*How* early?"

"We've made up lots of time flying on ten engines since Venus," Hugo told her, remembering having heard his parents discuss it.

"Why did no one tell me this?" Flo yelled, grabbing her maps off the shelf and switching on her computer.

"Would it have made any difference?" Hugo asked, sitting down beside her.

"There might still be time!" Flo exclaimed, doing some quick calculations.

"Time for what?" Hugo said, but Flo was too busy researching ingredients for the Perfect Pudding to hear him.

Trying to get her parents to fly through the Asteroid Belt to Planet Saturn took more persuasion than convincing them to ration the dry crackers.

"It's better to go straight to the Dog Bone," Jemima said when Flo suggested the idea. "At least we can rest there and save our energy for the Food and Fun Fest."

"There's no reason to go anywhere else," Hector said. "We've got our inventions ready. We'll get there early, get everything set up and just see how we get on."

But in the end Flo wore them out with her pleading and since they still felt bad about scoffing the bunch of bananas without offering her one, the auto pilot was set and the Potatis were off again.

When Flo read about Saturn's syrupy sprinkles she knew they were a must for the Perfect Pudding.

"The most satisfying crunch ever," she read to Hugo as he erased the Martian marshmallows from the top of his pancakes and revealed his idea about using a scented billboard to emit the aroma of the Perfect Pudding.

"But only if you're sure we've got time," he warned, watching his sister at her computer. "What shape are these sprinkles?"

"Spherical I think," Flo answered, studying the picture on the Space Web.

"Good!" Hugo smiled getting busy with his pencil. "Square would be too angular on the star fruit. But what if we get lost or something and end up missing the Food and Fun Fest altogether?"

"I agree … missing the Food and Fun Fest would be a far worse disaster than not having a crunchy topping," Flo said, printing off a map and switching off her computer, "But while there's still a chance to make the *perfect* pudding we can't give up."

11

On Pan

Flo stared in wonder at beautiful Planet Saturn as she polished off her meagre breakfast of four freeze-dried space berries. From a distance she had thought the rings looked like tiny balls stuck to the side of the planet, but now that they were approaching the edges of the outer ring she could see that the rings were giant cosmic hula hoops circling the golden sphere. And they weren't solid sheets of ice like she had first thought, but billions of icy moonlets ranging in size from a snowflake to an iceberg, each one orbiting Saturn like a miniature moon. There were even cosmic snowmen where a smaller snowball had stuck on top of a larger one.

"The origin of the rings is a mystery," Hector said, staring at the shimmering halo, but he was too hungry to enjoy it, and upset that the lump on his neck, the one he used for hanging his lab coat on, had fallen off during the night.

"Like the other rings in the Solar System they were probably moons that got smashed up by meteorites," Jemima said, stroking Hector's neck where the lump had been with one of her good hands and assuring him a bigger and better one would grow back one day.

As well as the icy moonlets, Hugo was fascinated to see that Saturn was host to a whole troop of moons.

"That's Titan," Jemima said, pointing to a giant globe as Flo sneaked off to load up the pod.

She counted seven groups of rings as she flew up and out of the spaceship. Snowballs fired at her from all directions as she weaved her way through a snowstorm. All the time she knew that if a chunk of ice hit her, it would be fatal. She glanced at her map. She had to find Pan, the tiny ice moon orbiting in one of the rings. Many of the rings had gaps where moons had caused them to split and, looking over to the dark side of the planet, she could see stars peeping through them. The gap between the third and fourth groups of rings was very wide. Then she spotted another much thinner gap, splitting the fourth group. According to the *Wingo,* Pan was somewhere in this gap. She flew over it at full speed until at last she spotted it clearing a pathway through the snowballs. She began her descent, dodging lumps of snow while maintaining control. The darkness was beginning to creep in, and very soon the little sunlight that there was would be gone. She had no time to waste.

The sudden icy chill made her shiver when she stepped out of the pod. Quickly she headed to the dome-shaped icehouse and entered the narrow tunnel of snow blocks. When she came to the swing doors she pushed them open and stepped inside.

"Good journey?" asked the cheerful looking Saturnian who pulled up a stool at the ice bar for her to sit on.

"Fine thanks," Flo smiled, eyeing up the ice sculptures around her. Everything was made of ice, even the cups and spoons, and the bar itself was a long, thin slab of ice.

"I would like some of your syrupy sprinkles without the slush," she said to the Saturnian who introduced herself as Jax, *the best slush-maker in the Universe*.

"*Without* slush?" Jax said in surprise.

"Yes, just the sprinkles, please," Flo smiled, staring at the big jar of sprinkles on the ice shelf.

"Sorry, they come together," Jax said in a matter-of-fact tone. "I make slush *with* sprinkles. No slush, no sprinkles … that's how it is."

"What about I take a little slush with lots of sprinkles?" Flo suggested, getting impatient with the rules at the ice bar.

"Why don't you try some?" Jax smiled, pouring her blue ice crystal drink into a cup and sprinkling the syrupy sprinkles on top.

Flo ran her tongue along the top of the slush until it was thickly coated with syrupy sprinkles. Then she began to crunch. Syrupy sprinkles were fabulous; sweet and crunchy with the most fantastic rich butterscotch flavour. They were even better than the marshmallows. She would take the slush for her family to enjoy and keep the sprinkles for the Perfect Pudding. Of course, that depended on one thing …

"I bet you would love this amazing, state-of-the-art *Dream Machine* that stores your dreams for replay when you wake up," she said to Jax, taking it out of the box and putting it on the ice bar.

"I don't sleep much these days," Jax yawned, wiping sticky splashes off the slush machine with her cloth and cleaning inside the nozzles. "I keep active to stay warm."

"What about as a present," Flo suggested trying to persuade her.

"For whom?" Jax asked, making herself a slush with sprinkles and guzzling it down.

"For your mother perhaps?" Flo said, showing her the headphones. "You know, this ability to see into the mind is one of the most brilliant advances in space technology."

"I don't see my mother," Jax sighed sadly. "She emigrated to a hot planet, somewhere in the Andromeda Galaxy. But I do have a brother," she said as an afterthought. "He sleepwalks."

"Perfect!" Flo laughed excitedly. "He'll be able to see where he went after he wakes up."

"How does it work exactly?" Jax said, putting down her cleaning cloth and pulling up a stool beside her.

"My mother invented it," Flo explained proudly. "You wear these special headphones with the in-built mini-camera and it captures the pictures in your brain while you sleep and stores them for replay on the monitor. You can watch them as soon as you wake up, or keep them for a later date when there's nothing much on Space TV."

"Okay," Jax said taking the *Dream Machine* from Flo and putting it behind her ice bar. "I just hope my brother walks to some interesting places."

Flo was elated. It was the easiest trade yet.

With the jar of sprinkles and tub of slush stuffed under her seat she flew up and over the icehouse. But she wasn't concentrating like she usually did. She was thinking about the Perfect Pudding and the addition of the amazing syrupy crunch to the rest of the wonderful ingredients. And that was probably why she didn't see the meteorites. When the first one clipped the side of the pod hurling it into the icy moonlets she was thrown out of her seat, and when the second one hit the front window a huge flame shot out of the control panel.

Desperately, she searched for something to extinguish the fire. But there was nothing. The pod was starting to fill up with smoke. She knew then she had no choice. She closed her eye and fought off tears as she stripped off the top layer of her skin. Her skin wasn't ready to come off yet, not for another month or so when it would fall off naturally and painlessly, leaving a layer of fresh new skin underneath. But the old skin was thick and strong and exactly what she needed to beat out the flames.

With the fire under control she grabbed the steering just as another meteorite crashed onto the roof propelling the pod into a huge chunk of ice. It was a disaster. She was caught in some kind of meteorite shower within Saturn's rings and the damage to the pod was now critical. As she spun out of control something walloped her head and something else whacked her cheek. When she saw the squashed star apple fruit and banana on the instrument panel she knew she had been lucky. If it had been a mango it would have knocked her head off.

Somehow she managed to regain control of the steering while ducking out of the way of the flying fruit. Recalling all her practice sessions on the flight simulator she skilfully flew the damaged pod up and out of the rings, blasting full speed ahead, flying from Saturn's frantic cloud tops until she arrived, shaken, at the fringes of the outer ring. Her body was raw and sore but it would soon heal. As the rings shimmered in the last few rays of sunlight she flew towards her spaceship. It was then she realised her foot was wet and there was a strange, sweet smell. She looked down in dismay. The container of pancake mix had spilled all over the floor of the pod and the crate of rainforest fruit was completely empty.

12

One Last Chance

Hovering above the spaceship Flo inspected the damage. Creamy white pancake mixture coated the entire length of the pod. Six star apple fruit were mashed into it and were unsalvageable. The rest had dents in them but were possibly usable. The mangoes and bananas were pretty much as they had been when picked, apart from being covered with sticky batter. It was a disaster.

The pancake, the most important ingredient, was gone. She had most of the fruit, but now no pancake to stuff or to sprinkle. It wouldn't even be a proper pudding, never mind a perfect pudding.

When she flew into the spaceship it was evident from the way her parents were leaning on to each other for support that they were getting much weaker. It was little wonder. They had given Hugo their share of freeze-dried space berries for breakfast and were desperate to get their hands on whatever she had brought back from her visit to Planet Saturn.

Flo knew when she opened the pod door they would see the sticky mess on the floor, but she wasn't sure that mattered any more. Hector would probably lick the floor and when he tasted the pancake batter and rainforest fruit he would know she had been hiding things from them. But Flo Potati had more determination than most nine-year-old Uzians, and for that reason she was not yet willing to divulge the ingredients for the Perfect Pudding.

"Get a long straw!" she yelled to Hugo through a hole in the door made by the impact of the meteorite.

Hugo ran to the kitchen and returned with the longest straw he could find in the kitchen cupboard.

"Put it through the hole," she instructed, pointing it out to him from the pod window, and no sooner had he inserted the straw than their parents were taking it in turns to suck Jax's icy blue slush until every last delicious drop was gone.

"Thank you, dear," Jemima smiled through the window of the pod.

"Yes, it was superb," Hector beamed. Neither he nor Jemima even bothered to ask why they had been drinking through a hole in the space pod door … which was really just as well.

Flo looked at the ingredients under her bed; the box of star apple fruit (some damaged), mangoes, bananas and syrupy sprinkles. It would hardly be the pudding of her dreams. It would be a liquid pudding or a purée with syrupy sprinkles. *Mashed Fruit with Sprinkles* she would call it. The can of volcano-smoked gas, wedged behind her seat at the time of the meteorite hits, would just go to waste. She sat down at her computer and stared miserably at the screen as Hugo opened his design pad. He had sketches of pancakes on every page, folded and rolled in every possible way. He had even started working on a twelve-sided pancake. Now all he had to work with was fruit and sprinkles, and it didn't matter how creative he was, it still looked like a big blob in the middle of the page.

"There might be one last chance," Flo mumbled, reading something she had found on the Space Web about an ingredient on Planet Jupiter.

"What are you talking about?" Hugo said, trying to spruce up his blobs.

"Val the volcanologist said *the secret's in the gas*, so if I can find something else to cook with the gas, I could still make the Perfect Pudding."

"Are you serious?" Hugo grinned looking at the pictures of mouth-watering doughnuts Flo was showing him. "We'll be late and you'll be lucky to get the spare pod after the damage you did to the other one."

"We're passing Jupiter on the way to the Dog Bone Asteroid anyway," Flo told him, printing off her map and weather charts and powering down her computer. "We'll make one final stop and I'm sure it won't be a problem convincing Mum and Dad to give me the pod if I promise to check the meteor forecast before I set off."

When Hector and Jemima came to Flo's bedroom to open her curtains in the morning it wasn't the first time they had found their son conked out on Flo's bedroom floor.

"You should try to use your bed, dear," Jemima scolded him, stepping over his long dangly legs to get to the window, "You're developing bad sleeping habits."

"Sorry," Hugo yawned pulling himself up.

It had been a particularly late-night planning session finalising advertising ideas for the Perfect Pudding. Free samples were definitely an option if things were slow on the day. The space mails to rouse curiosity about the Perfect Pudding were gone. The slogan *Perfection: It's arrived!* would be written in big bold writing and displayed above plates of the Perfect Pudding. Underneath the slogan in smaller writing it would say, *"The Perfect Pudding: A cosmic assortment of flavours from around the Milky Way."*

Hector's Inflatables were too risky and although using a scented billboard to emit the aroma of the Perfect Pudding was a fantastic idea, making one in the little time they had left was just not possible.

Hector and Jemima had been up early, boxing up all their inventions ready to lift on to the Dog Bone Asteroid. But Jupiter was their favourite planet in the Milky Way Galaxy and they wanted their children to see it.

"It's the whole Solar System in one place!" Hugo gasped, staring in amazement at the incredible view outside the window.

Flo was more prepared for the breathtaking sight having studied her maps. She knew Jupiter was *like* the whole Solar System, with the planet at the centre and all its moons, some planet-sized, orbiting around it. It even had its own asteroid collection *and* a ring. She studied the swirling patterns on Jupiter's face. Dotted amongst the orange and cream stripy clouds were storms, the most fearsome of which was the Great Red Spot. She could see it raging. It looked like the top of a giant volcano.

Hector and Jemima agreed to let Flo have a quick visit to Jupiter in the spare pod only because she promised to get something delicious to re-energise them for the Food and Fun Fest, and they needed all the energy they could get. But they had not agreed to let Hugo go with her so easily.

"You're a bit young, darling," Jemima said when he asked.

"You know the rules," Hector had insisted.

Hugo did know the rules. *"Nine is young enough to start flying pods,"* his parents always said. *"Parents who let their children start flying in pods younger than nine are irresponsible,"* they had repeated many times. But as Flo promised to stay in complete charge of the flying and guaranteed Hugo would find them a tasty snack even quicker than she would, they eventually gave in. Of course, Flo had her own reasons for wanting her brother to accompany her. She needed a co-pilot; someone to help navigate through the treacherous storms. Also, Jupiter was massive. The only thing bigger in the Solar System was the Sun itself. She needed all the help she could get.

She activated the anti-spin and Hugo and Flo Potati nose-dived at full speed towards the giant globe. Hugo knew the violent storms were a constant threat to their safety but he stayed focused, studying the weather charts and steering his sister away from the worst of them. In no time at all they were through the swirling clouds and flying through a hazy atmosphere. 600 kilometres, 700, 800 … on and on they flew. The massive headlamps that their father had fitted just before they left were on full beam, but they were now flying through thick gas and visibility was virtually zero. The outside temperature reading was 2,000 degrees and rising.

"I hope these doughnuts are worth it!" Hugo said, looking anxiously at his sister.

"They will be!" Flo smiled as the gas began to change into a shiny silver liquid.

They were now flying through what the *Wingo* called "a sea of hot churning metal" and the temperature and pressure gauges were so high they were on the blink.

"Get ready for the power down," Flo commanded studying her maps. "We're almost there."

"Where?" Hugo asked, staring blankly out of the window.

"At Jupiter's core," Flo beamed, slamming her foot on the brake.

13

The Final Ingredient

The gravitational pull of the core was strong, but with the brakes fully activated the pod's nose widened into a flat shield that slowed them down.

"Nice control!" Hugo smiled as Flo angled the flat shield through the liquid metal. But the liquid was now so thick Flo was slicing her way through it. It was hard to believe they were at the centre of the giant planet ... at the core swamped by Jupiter's massive oceans.

"Lights!" Hugo yelled excitedly when he spotted them.

Flo had told him to look out for the door of the core and it was only now she knew for certain that her map was spot on. When the lights changed from red to green and a beam of brilliant white pierced the darkness they flew inside.

"Cool space pods!" Hugo smiled, pulling his notepad out to make some quick sketches of the designer vehicles that were parked all around them. But there was no time for that.

"Let's go!" Flo said excitedly, grabbing her brother's arm and rushing over to the lift.

They had three levels to choose from; *Radio Jupiter*, *Flight Control Centre* and *Space TV*. Flo hit button 3 for *Space TV* and up they went.

"Thank goodness you're here!" an exasperated-looking Jovian with a clipboard yelled when the lift stopped and they stepped out.

"I had absolutely no idea someone was expecting us," Flo said as the Jovian took them by the arm and led them into a room with "*Main Studio*" written above the door.

"Are you kidding?" the Jovian exclaimed in disbelief. "You're on in twenty minutes."

"On where?" Flo said in bewilderment.

"On TV, of course," the Jovian bawled, getting annoyed with them.

"Sorry, you've got us mixed up with someone else," Flo said apologetically.

"You're kidding, right?" the Jovian said almost in tears. "You mean you're *not* the actors from Io?"

"Actually … that depends," Flo muttered thoughtfully.

"Depends on what?" the Jovian asked in desperation.

"Have you got any doughnuts?" Flo said, sensing her chance.

"Doughnuts?" the Jovian repeated in surprise. "Are you hungry?"

"Starving!" Flo said rubbing her belly.

"Get these guys some doughnuts!" the Jovian shouted to anyone within earshot. "Get them five, ten … as many doughnuts as they want. Just tell them to hurry up and get into costume."

"I can't believe he thinks we're actors!" Hugo laughed, enjoying the mix-up as much as the design of the studio.

"If it gets us the doughnut dough we'll go through with it!" Flo whispered, "We can't depend on the box of inventions."

"I would like a bag of your special doughnuts," she said to the chef who came out of the kitchen to help, "And lots of doughnut dough too, please."

"Dough?" the chef asked puzzled.

"Just give them a tub of dough!" the Jovian with the clipboard yelled. "They've obviously got strange eating habits. Just give them what they want."

"Now what?" Hugo said when they had a bag of doughnuts and a giant tub of dough.

But it was too late for them to do anything. The make-up artist had come out of the dressing room and began dabbing sticky black paint all over Hugo's face.

"It's okay," the make-up artist said when Hugo looked surprised. "I'm just trying to make you look dirty. You know … like there's been an explosion."

And then came possibly the luckiest moment in the creation of the Perfect Pudding. Looking rather windswept, the real actors arrived just in time to shoot the latest episode of *Volcano Adventure,* apologising for getting lost in the Great Red Spot again. Before anyone had the chance to ask Flo and Hugo about the giant tub of doughnut dough they were off and running.

But Flo didn't feel too guilty about that. She would have helped them out if she had had to. After all, she had considered a career on the stage before finding her passion for cooking.

When they reached the turbulent liquid gas they knew they were more than half way there, and with a doughnut each to maximise their concentration for re-entry into the thick Jovian atmosphere they were almost home. Hugo directed his sister out of the night side of the planet, well away from the storms. Once more they flew over the ever-changing patterns of orange and cream clouds. With the last ingredient for the Perfect Pudding on-board, from beneath the most fearsome oceans in the Solar System, they bid the giant planet farewell and headed back to the spaceship … to their parents, who had started firing up the engines ready to blast them to the Food and Fun Fest.

But the engines weren't firing, and no one was going anywhere.

14

Going Nowhere

"Anyone for doughnuts?" Flo yelled, leaping out of the space pod. Their parents were nowhere to be seen. They were normally waiting; desperate to snatch whatever she had found.

"What's going on?" she shouted when she ran into the control room and found them trying to jump-start the main engine with the emergency solar power pack.

"It fell off …" Jemima sniffled, trying desperately to fix the problem, "Right into the mechanisms, jamming everything up."

"What fell off?" Flo asked, putting the bag of doughnuts on the table.

"His lower ear," Jemima sobbed, peering down at the engine to see if she could spot it and yank it back out.

"It will have been pulverised by now," Flo exclaimed in panic, "Chopped into hundreds of little pieces. Everything will be clogged up."

"You should have been prepared for it happening," Jemima scolded her husband as she continued to search for the missing ear. "It's been dangling from your neck for weeks."

"I'm sorry," Hector apologised. "I tried to catch it but it slid right through my fingers."

"It's no use," Jemima cried, trying over and over again to get things moving.

"It's kaput," Hector groaned. "We've even downloaded up-to-the minute technical advice for spaceship malfunctions, but it's all hopeless."

"Have you tried all ten engines?" Flo asked, helping her mother re-try the power pack.

"All ten engines have been checked and tried," Jemima assured her.

"Would anyone like a doughnut?" Hugo suggested, trying to stay calm while offering the bag first to his father and then to his mother. But for the first time in four million light years they had all lost their appetites.

"We've got to get there," Flo whispered to Hugo. "We've got everything we need for the Perfect Pudding, and what happens? Dad's ear falls in to the main engine and we break down."

"Is that all you can think about?" Hugo snapped bursting into tears. "We might die."

"Everything will be okay, darling," Jemima said, drying her own tears and holding her son in her arms.

"It's my fault," Flo said, sitting down with her head in her hands. "If I hadn't persuaded everyone to journey to more planets, we would be there already, setting out all our inventions, waiting for the Food and Fun Fest to begin."

Hugo looked miserably at his sister. He knew she was probably right.

"If only we had something to kick start the engines," Hector said rummaging in all the cupboards, "We need a surge of power to get things going."

And that was when Flo thought about the volcano-smoked gas. She knew it might work. It might not, but they had to try everything they had. If they didn't they could be stranded for years, possibly light years, before their spaceship was discovered, and by that time there wouldn't be an arm, or a leg, or even a toe left to show for the Potati space travellers. She also knew if they used the volcano-smoked gas it would be the end of the Perfect Pudding and her dream of nonstop space travel.

"Try this," Flo said, handing her father her precious can of volcano-smoked gas.

"Where did this come from?" Hector exclaimed, staring in surprise at the gas and yelling to his wife to come and see.

"Never mind where she got it!" Jemima cried excitedly. "Try it!"

Flo watched tentatively as her father carefully attached the volcano-smoked gas to the main engine and popped the can.

Immediately and miraculously Hector's ear shot out of the engine and the spaceship roared into life.

"We're off!" Hector laughed, hugging Flo and jumping for joy around the control room.

"That's great," Flo said, staring vacantly at the empty can on the spaceship floor beside the shrivelled ear.

15

A Change of Plan

"What are you up to now?" Hugo said when he came to his sister's bedroom expecting to find her staring miserably out of the window, but instead found her tinkering with the big old oven that usually sat at the back of their store room.

"I've had a brainwave," Flo said, tightening up the hinges on the oven door and checking the dials were all in working order.

"Yes?" Hugo said wanting to finish his final sketches of *mashed fruit with sprinkles*.

"Instead of using gas to deep-fry the doughnuts as planned, I'm going to oven-bake them for the Perfect Pudding."

"Bake them?" Hugo said, looking at his sister in surprise. "But will they taste as good?"

"They'll be even *better* than fried doughnuts," she assured him, "Light and fluffy and even more tempting because they'll be healthy too."

"So, the Perfect Pudding's back on!" Hugo smiled, putting a big line through *mashed fruit with sprinkles* in his sketch pad and turning to a new page.

"It certainly is!" Flo laughed, stuffing her tool bag into her drawer. "I'm not going to let some gas spoil my plans."

She had the perfect ingredients; succulent rainforest fruit from Earth, amazing oven-baked doughnuts from Jupiter, and sensational syrupy sprinkles with their rich butterscotch flavour from Saturn's icy moon. Now, with the help of her designer, they had to decide the best way to present it on a plate.

"The striking star pattern shouldn't be hidden under sprinkles," Hugo said showing Flo his first sketch.

"I agree," Flo smiled, "A light sprinkle will be enough."

"And don't sprinkle everything," Hugo insisted. "Only sprinkle the slices of star apple fruit on the doughnut. The smooth purée at the side will be a clever contrast."

"How are you going to make the holes in the doughnuts?" Hugo asked when the thought entered his head.

"I'll poke them out with my finger," Flo grinned.

"No!" Hugo said horrified at the thought of misshapen holes.

"Only kidding!" Flo laughed. "I've got the cutters ready; one doughnut-sized cutter and one small cutter guaranteeing a perfect hole every time."

"Fancy trying some oval holes?" Hugo suggested, doing a quick sketch of a doughnut with an oval hole in it and showing it to his sister.

"Why do you always have to complicate things?" Flo smiled, watching her brother at work.

"I wouldn't be a designer if I didn't come up with the ideas!" Hugo laughed, closing his sketch pad and rushing to the control room to join his parents. He had just spotted the Asteroid Belt through the window.

The Dog Bone Asteroid had been picked to host the Food and Fun Fest because of its unusual shape, but it was *still* tricky to find.

"I remember once there was a delay getting the show on the road," Hector recalled, dodging out of the way of a massive triangular-shaped asteroid while holding onto his loose leg.

"What happened?" Hugo asked, watching his parents skilfully navigate their spaceship through the massive loop of rocks.

"The asteroid that previously hosted the Food and Fun Fest was sucked away by Jupiter's gravitational pull," Hector said, anticipating the cone-shaped asteroid playing Follow my Leader with a band of cratered chunks.

"It was bad timing for Zak Nutt who had got there early to set up shop," Jemima recollected, having read all about the Martian's misfortunes in the *Cosmic Gazette*.

"He was a bit of a nut anyway!" Hector joked, remembering his legendary catapult invention that had backfired and given him a black eye.

"That's beside the point, dear," Jemima said to her husband, while supporting his leg with her limp arm.

Flo was fascinated by the band of drifting rocks tumbling along outside, some no more than tiny pebbles, while others could flatten a whole country on Planet Earth if they plummeted in that direction.

"Where did they all come from?" she asked as her parents steered the spaceship around a giant cube-shaped asteroid.

"Possibly leftovers from when all the planets were formed," Jemima answered, letting out a sigh of relief now that the giant cube was visible in the rear-view mirror.

"Or the asteroids might have *been* a planet that got smashed into millions of pieces when it collided with a huge comet," Hector said, recalling something he had read on the Space Web.

Whatever their origin they all agreed that the unique mini-moons formed a beautiful chunky belt wrapping itself around the Solar System, separating the rocky planets from the gas giants.

Flo's eye never left the asteroids and after a while she began to feel quite dizzy. Her parents were totally focused, re-energised by the last two doughnuts in the bag. It had been easiest at the outer edge of the asteroid belt, where the rocks were further apart and they could anticipate their moves and weave their way in. But the further they went, and as the number of rocks increased, the trickier it became. The large chunks of rock were easiest to avoid, but many of the small ones were just too tricky to get around and clattered off the spaceship before continuing their long, slow journey.

It was Hugo who eventually spotted the Dog Bone Asteroid through his telescope.

"That's it!" he yelled, "Looking more dog-bone-shaped than ever."

A huge crowd was expected following advice on Asteroid TV to get there early or miss out on a trading bay. The Food and Fun Fest would begin in the morning and Flo Potati wouldn't sleep a wink. The magnitude of the day had just hit her and she was starting to worry. She had thought up the Perfect Pudding but she had not actually tried making it.

What if the combination of flavours was not as fantastic as she imagined it would be? What if the fruit had lost its freshness or the oven packed in? It *was* old. Would the mixture of soft and crunchy textures in the pudding be a winning contrast?

She lay in bed watching the Dog Bone Asteroid fill with spaceships under the cold rocky sky as Hugo painted the words *"Perfection: It's Arrived!"* on his advertising banner. She looked at the words and at the boxes of ingredients stacked up by her bedroom door, trying not to think about long, boring days without space travel because they didn't have enough food or energy to travel the galaxies. Everything rested on this one attempt to make the *perfect* pudding.

The ingredients were checked and ready to go.

The design was final.

16

The Food and Fun Fest

From the second Jemima yelled, "Breakfast's ready! Come and get it," it was all go in the Potati spaceship. Jemima's space-fruit plant had produced a few fruits in the night and they gobbled them down with the last four crackers in the packet.

Flo had been watching the activities from her bedroom window feeling surprisingly calm. She was amazed at the number of spaceships parked along the entire length of the Bone, with even more squashed into the bulbous ends. Some families were still arriving, trying to negotiate a good landing spot, and Flo knew they would be lucky to get one. There weren't many spaces left, or at least good spaces where you could easily display your inventions or food stuffs, or whatever you had to trade at the Food and Fun Fest.

But when she stepped out of the spaceship onto the rocky ground of the Dog Bone Asteroid she started to worry. She had to ensure the Perfect Pudding was a success and that was why she got ratty when Hector asked her to carry boxes of inventions out of the spaceship.

"I *have* to get cooking," she snapped, ignoring her father and lifting out crates and tubs and boxes of cooking utensils onto the rocky asteroid ground.

"*What* did you say?" Hector asked, trying to peer through the lids.

"Just wait and see," Flo said, showing Hugo where to stack everything.

"Did I hear you say you had to get cooking?" Jemima exclaimed, dragging all five of her legs off the spaceship.

It was lucky for the existence of the Perfect Pudding that everyone was suddenly distracted by Mrs Jag from Titan who had spotted their spaceship and come over to welcome them to the Dog Bone Asteroid. But when she spotted Hector she let out a gasp.

"You look awful," she said peering at where Hector's ears had been and at his shrivelled cone-shaped chin.

"It's been a difficult year," Jemima said, trying to hide her curled chin with her good hand. "We ran out of food and didn't find too many friendly planets to top up our supplies."

"Really?" Mrs Jag exclaimed having a closer look at Hector's chin. "You should have planned better."

"Hector's been amazing," Jemima said, ignoring Mrs Jag's impolite comments and giving her husband a big hug. "He had less so that the children and I could have more."

"Actually, you're not looking so great yourself," Hector said to nosey Mrs Jag when he got fed up with her staring at his face.

"I beg your pardon," Mrs Jag huffed in her posh tones. "I've had the best beauty treatments this year."

"I would never have known," Jemima muttered, side-stepping snooty Mrs Jag and rushing over to say hello to her friend Lex, when she spied her trendy red spaceship parked neatly between the two black, exclusive spaceships belonging to the Neptune brothers, Tiz and Wiz. When Jemima had got married Lex had carried her good luck charm; a large meteorite sculpted into the shape of a cat. Lex's arms had never recovered.

"How are your arms"? Hector called to Lex after some chit-chat with the Neptune brothers about their technologically advanced flying machines.

"Good days and bad days," Lex smiled, holding up her left arm with her right hand to show how the muscles hadn't fully healed.

There wasn't any time for small talk. Tins of tangerine and olive paint were stacked on top of the *Smelly- and Tasty-Visions*. *Hector's Beards* were neatly trimmed and hung from a shelf behind them. Most of the beards were white so the five black ones would no doubt be the first to go. Hector had sculpted heads from chunks of rock to show how to wear the beards … either on your chin or your head. The *Zapa-Snapas* were all charged up ready to demonstrate invisibility with one zap. The *Dream Machine* took prime position on a table in front of everything else. Jemima was hoping to demonstrate it throughout the day, but the chance of falling asleep with all the swapping of foodstuffs or inventions or whatever was unlikely. Boxes of *Paper with Flavour* were stacked up nearby and the *Sucking and Sorting Hoovers* were on display beside them.

It was when Hector was using a foot pump to blow up an *Inflatable Spare Room with Clean Towels for Visitors* that he spotted Flo and Hugo dragging the big old oven off the spaceship.

"Nobody's going to want *that* old thing!" he laughed.

"You're probably right," Flo grinned, placing it between their two tables. Hugo had decided they needed two tables; one to make the Perfect Pudding and the other to display it. The boxes of cooking utensils and ingredients would stay on the ground until needed.

"Remember to slice the star apple fruit just thick enough to show off the star pattern," Flo insisted when Hugo got busy with the knife, while she began peeling bananas and chopping mangoes.

"Don't worry!" Hugo smiled, enjoying slicing the sweet-smelling fruits, before passing the rest to Flo for the rainforest purée.

When Flo switched on her blender they watched in delight as the red pulp mixed with the banana and melon to make the striking orange rainforest purée.

The oven was at exactly the right baking temperature when she began flattening the doughnut dough with her rolling pin, and when she was satisfied it was the thickness she wanted she punched out the doughnut-sized holes while Hugo worked with the smaller cutter. They had only just put the first batch of doughnuts into the oven when Hector's noses began to twitch in their direction.

"Can you smell that?" he cried to Jemima, who was yanking the lid off the paint with her sharp nails to show the colour.

Hector became so excited by the delicious aroma that his foot began pumping in triple time and an *Inflatable Spare Room with Clean Towels for Visitors* burst with a BANG!

Jemima screamed. "Please concentrate, dear," she scolded. "We can't afford to waste any inventions."

"Sorry," Hector said apologetically, "But I can smell something and it's driving me bonkers."

Funnily enough, Jemima's noses were starting to twitch too. They had both been so busy setting everything up that they hadn't paid any attention to what their children were doing, but when they realised the delicious smell was coming from the big old oven they were over in a flash.

"What's going on here?" Hector demanded, slamming his foot pump on the table and staring at Hugo mounting his banner above the tables.

"I'm making something," Flo said, trying to block their view of the oven. But it was impossible for her to hide everything now.

"Do you mean to tell me you've had *these* in the spaceship while my noses have been shrinking and my chin has been curling?" Jemima exclaimed, holding up a bunch of bananas.

"It was for the best," Flo insisted, yanking the jug of rainforest purée from her father's hands and giving him and Jemima a banana to share.

Luckily for the Perfect Pudding the Food and Fun Fest had just begun and Hector and Jemima's first customer was demanding attention. When the doughnuts were golden brown Flo lifted them expertly onto the plates. Hugo placed slices of star apple fruit on top while Flo drizzled the rainforest purée and sprinkled the sprinkles.

"Let's taste it!" Hugo smiled handing his sister a plate.

But Flo just beamed triumphantly at the Perfect Pudding.

"It has everything a pudding should have and more," she said, looking at each of the fantastic ingredients in turn, and remembering how hard she had worked to get them.

"Are you ready then?" Hugo said about to dig in with his spoon.

"I am!" Flo smiled.

And that was when *their* first customer, who had been eyeing up the puddings, shouted for attention.

"Can I help you?" Flo said putting down her spoon.

"Yes!" the customer said, sniffing a pudding. "It says on this banner here that you're serving up the Perfect Pudding today, and I want to know *why* it is perfect."

"If you taste it you'll find out," Flo said confidently, pulling out a tray of doughnuts from the oven and praising her brother for the colourful banner and slogan he had made to advertise it.

"I'll take one in return for my multi-vitamin pasta," the customer said, giving a box of pasta to Hugo and helping himself to a plate.

Flo and Hugo watched as he took a spoonful of the Perfect Pudding.

"I think he likes it!" Hugo laughed, watching his spoon fly between the pudding and his mouth.

"It looks like it!" Flo smiled, waiting for the customer to say something.

"I have never, ever, tasted anything quite like this," he said eventually, when he had scoffed the lot and his tongue had recovered from the explosion of flavours. "The combination of ingredients in this pudding is out of this world."

"That's because they *are* out of this world!" Flo smiled, slicing more star apple fruit and passing the tub of sprinkles to Hugo.

"What do you mean?" the customer said, handing another box of pasta to Hugo and taking another pudding.

So Flo started to tell him about her quest to find the ingredients for the ultimate cosmic experience.

"You mean this piece is from Earth?" he said nibbling the star apple fruit. "It's amazing! And with these syrupy sprinkles from Saturn it's a winner! Are there more ingredients as sensational as these out there?" he asked watching Flo and Hugo at work.

"Oh yes!" Flo exclaimed, drizzling the rainforest purée on the plates. "The Perfect Pudding is just the tip of the iceberg."

"Really?" the customer said, reaching into his jacket pocket and pulling out a notebook and pencil.

"As a matter of fact," Flo declared, "I've just read about a delicious sweet spice unique to Pluto, and Neptune and Uranus have exceptional ingredients that I can't wait to get my hands on. In fact, I hope to create the Marvellous Muffin next."

"I love it!" the customer cried excitedly, "… using ingredients from around the Solar System to create a taste sensation! It's phenomenal!"

"I am rather pleased with it!" Flo grinned, looking proudly at the Perfect Pudding.

"So you should be, young … sorry, what did you say your name was?"

"I didn't," Flo pointed out. "But it's Flo … Flo Potati."

"Well, young Flo, I have an offer for you," he said, writing everything down in his notebook. "I work at Star Excel, the number one cooking college in the Universe, and I am inviting you to come and study to be a top chef."

"Are you serious?" Flo said switching off her blender. "That's my dream."

"Well, you've obviously got what it takes," he said, handing Flo his space mail address. "We're always on the lookout for talented youngsters who go the extra mile for what they believe in."

"When can I start?" Flo asked, looking at the address in her hand and at Hugo, who was watching her.

"My brother was the designer and advertising consultant," she explained, putting her arm around Hugo, oblivious to everyone who was queuing up for a taste of the Perfect Pudding.

"You're very good too," he said to Hugo, scribbling in his notebook again.

But Flo knew seven was too young to start college. Her parents would never allow her brother to go.

"You should go!" Hugo said, smiling proudly at his sister. "It's what you've always wanted."

"I could," Flo grinned thoughtfully, "But you know, I don't think I want to go to college *yet*."

"*Really?*" the customer said in amazement.

"Yes," Flo said, scooping out dough with her long, green fingers and getting busy with her rolling pin. "I want to travel some more with my family, uncover more fabulous ingredients. *Then* I'll come to Star Excel."

"Well, the place is yours, so come whenever you're ready," he said, licking his plate clean with his long, forked tongues.

17

The Proof of the Pudding

"*Now* can we taste the Perfect Pudding?" Hugo laughed, handing his sister a plate.

"You bet!" Flo grinned, cutting a chunk of doughnut with her spoon and putting it into her mouth. The fresh flavour of the fruit, the moist and tender texture of the doughnut and the sweet butterscotch flavour of the syrupy sprinkles was the taste sensation she had set out to find.

"Perfect!" she smiled savouring every bite, crunch and combination of flavours.

Flo Potati had given herself the ultimate cooking challenge, to make a pudding that was perfect. And she had done it. But she couldn't ignore the rest of her customers any longer.

"The Perfect Pudding!" Mrs Jag declared staring at the puddings and mulling over Hugo's sign. "*A cosmic assortment of flavours from around the Milky Way,*" she read out loud. "I've been intrigued ever since I got your space mail and I'm rather peckish so I'll trade a box of my delectable ravioli for one of your perfect puddings," she said to Flo.

Flo liked ravioli, but she had seen Mrs Jag trade with her parents for pots of tangerine and olive paint and wasn't sure how much ravioli one family could stand. Then again, she knew she shouldn't be fussy because it *was* possible to live off ravioli. She had even heard of a family who had lived off macaroni until it sprouted from their ears. She took the box of ravioli and watched Mrs Jag take a spoonful of the Perfect Pudding and put it into her mouth. Hugo was looking too, waiting to see what Mrs Jag thought about the cocktail of exotic ingredients.

Neither of them could ever have predicted her reaction to one taste of the Perfect Pudding in a million orbits of the Sun.

"What *is* she doing?" Flo muttered to Hugo in astonishment.

"Dancing, I think!" Hugo laughed, watching Mrs Jag hopping around and shaking her hips.

"I feel younger … invigorated!" Mrs Jag yelled to Mr Jag, who dropped his boxes of ravioli on his toes at the sight of his wife leaping about on the stony ground of the Dog Bone Asteroid.

Over at Hector and Jemima's tables things were not going quite so well. They had discovered that the *Zapa-Snapas* could be dangerous if they fell into the wrong hands.

"How could you have been so silly?" a Jovian was heard scolding her son who had zapped their spaceship, making it invisible so another one had landed on top of it.

"I just wanted to see if it worked," her son insisted, staring aghast at their squashed spaceship as the invisibility started to wear off.

"It worked all right," the Jovian grumbled. "And you'll pay for the damage," she yelled at Hector and Jemima, shaking her fists in fury and grabbing back her long-life bread rolls.

When a customer from Charon, Pluto's icy moon, took *his* first spoonful of the Perfect Pudding he began to kiss it.

"Mamma mia!" he yelled excitedly, leaping over the table to kiss Flo.

"Steady on!" Flo laughed, ducking out of the way of the big, sticky lips heading her way.

"I think *he* likes it too!" Hugo laughed, putting the space-berry jam and long-life bread beside Mrs Jag's ravioli.

Things had picked up for Hector and Jemima. After everyone was clear about what to do with them, the beards traded well, especially with the ladies who were delighted to have something stylish and warm to wear on their trips to Pluto. They walked off admiring their new looks; curly black beards on their chin and white ones on their head. Their husbands were thrilled. But their success was short-lived when Jemima was demonstrating the *Smelly- and Tasty-Visions* and a documentary came on about the discovery of mummified aliens on Venus.

"Is that you, dear?" a Martian was heard whispering to her husband when there was the most horrendous stink, and the husband was so embarrassed that he convinced his wife not to trade, so Hector and Jemima had to wave goodbye to the freeze-dried dumplings.

They had some success with the *Dream Machine* though. When Hector dozed off during a lull in the trading Jemima took her chance and rigged him up. Luckily Hector was having one of his more exciting dreams about sleeping on top of a giant pancake dome on Venus, when it exploded throwing hot sticky jam into the atmosphere. A Saturnian was delighted with the funny sight of Hector flying through the sky wearing his polka-dot pyjama bottoms, and when they fell down she laughed so much she cried.

Flo and Hugo could hardly keep up with the demand for the Perfect Pudding, making it a most memorable year for the Potati family on the Dog Bone Asteroid.

Everyone who tried the unique taste sensation loved it and, before long, Flo and Hugo had enough food supplies to ensure they could continue with their space travels and orbit the whole galaxy a hundred times if they wanted. Which was really just as well because even though their parents managed to trade most of the *Paper with Flavour,* the *Sucking and Sorting Hoovers* and the *Inflatable Spare Rooms with Clean Towels for Visitors* just didn't do very well at all.

"Flo, Hugo …? Where are you?" Jemima called as they walked over to their children's tables to break the terrible news that, without adequate food supplies, space travel was now too risky.

But the strange thing was … there were so many boxes and crates piled up on their children's tables that they couldn't even *see* them. Hector began to examine the labels. "Giant ravioli, four large bags of multi-vitamin pasta, space-berry jam and a pallet of long-life bread, ten packs of nutritious vacuum-packed sausages, bags of freeze-dried ice cream bars, ten barrels of long-life juice and one hundred tins of soup (assorted flavours)," he read in astonishment. And those were only the boxes and crates on the table. Jemima was examining the labels on the boxes *under* the table.

"Heaps of bakery products, drums of cereals, dried fruit by the bucket load, pots of herbs, spices and seasonings, masses of nuts and seeds, tubs of beans and peas, and oodles of noodles," she said in amazement.

"Would anyone like to try the Perfect Pudding?" Flo laughed when she saw the amazed look on her parents' faces.

"Don't mind if I do!" Hector exclaimed, snatching a plate off Flo and polishing it off in record time. Then there was no stopping him as he kicked off his shoes and grabbed his wife for a hokey-cokey.

"I never knew you were such a great mover!" Jemima laughed, stroking the lump on her husband's neck that had reappeared even bigger and better after eating the Perfect Pudding.

"I'll be able to hang two coats on it," Hector said excitedly.

"Possibly three, darling," Jemima smiled. "I think she gets her talent from my side of the family," Jemima laughed, looking at her daughter proudly, who was standing beside the mound of boxes and crates.

"I think you're probably right!" Hector grinned.

Not only had she secured space travel for herself and her family for another year, but Flo Potati had also secured herself a place at Star Excel to be trained by the best chefs in the Universe, and she would go when the time was right for her. She had looked beyond the empty kitchen cupboards and found her dream.

The Dog Bone Asteroid had been a great host for the Food and Fun Fest, but it was time for the asteroid to get back to its own travels. One by one the spaceships rose up into the band of drifting rocks. Hector took control of the spaceship and Flo headed off to the kitchen. With her top-notch designer and advertising consultant, Hugo, she had a lot of planning to do before they arrived at Planet Uranus and the start of her search for the finest ingredients for the Marvellous Muffin.

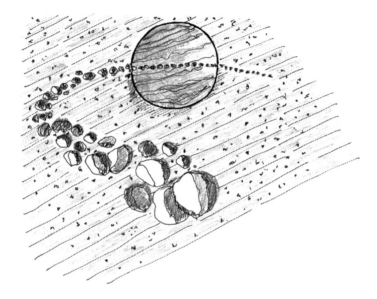

The Asteroids

Dream Machine

To the Dog Bone Asteroid

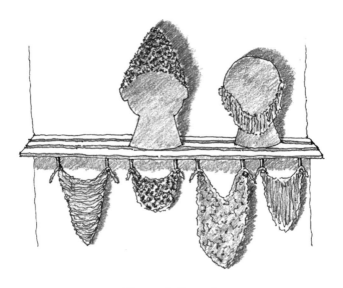

Hector's Beards

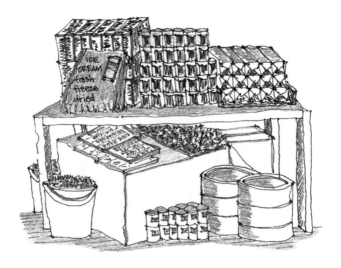

Didn't they do well!

The Perfect Pudding

Something to think about...........

What would be your perfect pudding and what planets and moons would you visit to get the ingredients?

Did you know there are maps of planets and moons? I found a great one of Mars in Edinburgh library.

Jupiter and Saturn have lots and lots of moons. Sponde, Arche, Kale, Atlas, Mimas, Phoebe and Skoll are just a few of them.

It's lucky this story is set in the future when instant translation devices make communication easy. Imagine the problems Flo could have encountered if no one understood Uzian.

Hector and Jemima are running out of ideas for inventions. Got any?

And finally, for those of you who don't like puddings .... plan your perfect sandwich!